As a Matter of Effect

By Ben Winter

As a Matter of Effect

By Ben Winter

Published by Success Improv, Colorado, USA

ISBN: 979-8-9895476-7-8

For inquiries, contact: https://mrimprov.com

Author's Note

Writing this book was an unexpected journey. It began heading in one direction, but—like most of my stories—it veered off the path I had planned. That's part of the magic for me. If I could predict every twist and turn, I'd lose interest. The surprises keep me engaged, and hopefully, they do the same for you.

To make this one work, I had to stretch into something unfamiliar—territory I hadn't written in before. But that's what keeps it fresh. If I'm not having fun or being challenged, I know the story won't land the way I want it to.

I owe so much to my writing family—those who support not just the stories, but the wild, unpredictable process of getting them onto the page. Chris, you're the first one I go to for feedback, insight, or just gut checks. You're such a damn good writer that it still blows my mind you enjoy my work. Unless, of course, you've been lying to me all along... in which case, keep it up. It's working.

To my love, Tara—thank you for cheering me on, for giving me the space to chase these characters and plotlines, and maybe enjoying the quiet while I do. It's a win-win.

As I write this, people close to me are going through deep losses. It's a stark reminder that life is short and precious. If you've ever had the urge to write, please don't wait. Start. Keep going. Tell your story. We don't get forever, but we do get this moment.

Thanks for taking the time to read mine.

—Ben.

CHAPTER 1

"And that… does it! Holepunch ready to go," Tericia says, her voice trembling with a mix of exhaustion and awe.

She steps back from the console, her pale fingers still hovering in the air like she's afraid a stray gesture might unravel everything. Under the harsh glowing lights, her skin looks nearly translucent—she hasn't seen the sun in ages. Her long brown hair, twisted into a loose ponytail, is fraying at the edges, and her lab coat hangs off her thin frame like it belongs to someone else. She hasn't eaten properly in days, but that's always been the trade—focus over food, work over sleep. Progress over everything.

"Yeah," Lester says, arms folded, expression unreadable. "That should be it. But we've got six weeks before we can even think about testing it."

He stands a few feet away, guarded, watching her with a calm that masks the storm always brewing behind his eyes. Lester's face is smooth-shaven, his dark skin making him look far younger than his forty-two years suggest. His neatly cropped hair is immaculate, as always. Reserved and precise, Lester rarely says more than he needs to. He wears his quiet like armor. But Tericia knows—his silence isn't peace. It's fear.

Tericia exhales hard, shoulders sagging. "You always did know how to kill my high."

"I'm just stating the facts."

"Yeah? Well, stop." She turns toward him, eyes narrowed, the glow of the display flickering across her face. "You never learned when to shut up and let a moment live. You always have to correct, to remind, to prove a point—even when it doesn't matter."

Lester raises his hands in a silent concession. He knows better than to argue, especially now.

"I get it," she mutters, raking a hand through her hair. "We can't test it here. Not on this planet. Hell, not even in this solar system. Not until we're damn sure hypothesis matches reality."

"You don't have to tell me. I wrote the initial framework for the containment field. Ran every simulation myself—" He stops mid-sentence, then lets out a quiet chuckle. "Oh. I see it now."

"Yeah," Tericia says, softening just a little. "We're both guilty of preaching to the converted."

She presses her palms into her eyes, then lets out a long yawn. The fatigue isn't just physical—it's baked into her bones.

"You need sleep," Lester says gently, concern threading his voice.

"I need a lobotomy," she mutters. "To erase this past week. Or month. Or hell, maybe the entire last year. This whole cursed project."

"What?"

She straightens. "I said, not until I put in the request for a ship. I want zero delays once the green light hits."

Lester frowns. "Right."

He drifts toward his terminal, fingers twitching like they miss the keys already. "Fine. I'll log the final dataset, then call it a day."

"That's not how it works anymore," Tericia says, watching him carefully.

"What do you mean?"

"Once we confirm readiness, everything gets locked down. Nobody touches it—not even us. Security steps in, seals the lab. We're off-limits until launch. Oh, and we will be moved to a more secure location."

Lester blinks. "Since when?"

She taps her temple, trying to recall. Then snaps her fingers. "That's right. You weren't at that meeting. I tried to find you after, but you weren't here. I got distracted. Then everything snowballed and I forgot."

Lester stiffens. "So what happens if I realize there's a flaw? Something I missed in the stabilizer phase? You know how often solutions come to me when I'm dreaming."

"I do," Tericia says, voice softer. "But if anything pops up, you'll have to write it down. Review it once we're enroute."

"I hate this."

She nods slowly. "Me too. But that's the cost of being funded. They make the rules."

Her voice drops, shame creeping in like fog. Lester doesn't push her. He just watches her for a long moment, then lets his gaze fall to the floor. He knows what she is thinking. What she is feeling.

"Borvil wants it to succeed," she says after a pause. "They want to protect it from sabotage, from last-minute interference. From us, even."

"That's insulting," Lester snaps. "As if either one of us would take a bribe or sabotage our dream."

"I know. You know. But they don't take chances. Remember?"

Lester nods reluctantly. "Yeah. I remember."

For a moment, silence blankets the room—thick, weary, almost reverent. The machine hums behind them, dormant for now, but heavy with potential. They've built something extraordinary. Dangerous. Beautiful.

"We'll have six weeks with it, out there," Lester murmurs. "Six weeks to study, tweak, maybe even perfect it. Hopefully."

"With guards watching our every move. Corporate auditors hovering. They won't let us breathe without checking our CO_2 levels," Tericia quips, but it lacks her usual fire.

"This better work," Lester mutters, rubbing the back of his neck. "Because I'm not getting shot by some intern with a clipboard over a misinterpreted variable."

Tericia laughs, a small, genuine thing. "You always said the real danger wasn't the science. It was the idiots funding it."

"Still true. Proven time and time again."

She leans back against the console. "Well, it comes with the funding," she says, trying to justify the last ten years.

Lester sighs. "I'm done for tonight. Since we are going to be moving to a "secure" location, I'm going to the sleeping quarters they so generously labeled a 'domicile' and drink myself into dreamless sleep until we leave."

"You'll have to stay drunk for a week, then," Tericia says, trying for levity. "I think it will take that long until we launch."

"It's a possibility." He turns toward the door.

"Lester," she calls out, voice suddenly urgent.

He pauses at the threshold. "Yeah?"

She hesitates, then says, "I'm proud of us. No matter what happens next… we figured it out. We made something real. The future will remember this moment."

He meets her gaze. Nods once, slowly. Then disappears into the corridor.

The lab feels colder without him. Quieter. Tericia wraps her arms around herself, staring at the dormant machine.

"I just wish the rest of the team was here to see it too," she whispers.

Then, in the hum of the silence, she lowers her head—and lets the moment pass.

CHAPTER 2

A day later, Tericia steps into the ship's loading corridor and pauses, turning her head just enough to catch a final glimpse of Earth through the hangar door. The blue skies of the planet hang overhead, silent and untouchable—home. And yet, her gaze might also be a final goodbye.

Behind her, footsteps. "Everything okay?" Lester asks.

She nods but doesn't look away. "Yes. It's fine. I just wasn't expecting us to leave this quickly. And I…"

"Don't know if we'll make it back?" he finishes gently.

Tericia glances at him, then nods again. "That… and everything we're leaving behind. Everyone…"

Lester follows her gaze. "I understand. But try to imagine what's ahead. It's the only way I'm able to step onto this ship."

"GET MOVING!" a voice bellows from inside.

Stan. Always too loud, too eager.

Lester rolls his eyes, then gestures toward the entrance with a crooked smile. Tericia exhales and takes lead up the ramp.

"Make me wait again and I'll punch you in the leg!" Stan threatens as they pass.

"Lay off, asshole," comes a gravelly voice behind him. "You'll do no such thing."

Grundle steps into view, massive and unshakable, his tone low and final. "This isn't that kind of assignment. And if you make my job harder by being a dick for six weeks, I won't just break your legs—I'll make you walk it off outside."

Stan's mouth moves but no sound comes. He lowers his head, sullen and quiet.

"Forgive him," Grundle mutters to Tericia and Lester as they pass. "He's new. Trained to bark orders, not assist innovators."

"It's fine," Tericia says with a sigh. "Nothing we haven't dealt with for the last decade."

Lester says nothing. He walks past both men without a glance, already halfway to disappearing into the ship's narrow spine.

The hatch seals shut behind them, the thud echoing like a heartbeat.

Tericia heads straight to her room and collapses onto the stiff bed. The hum of engines, low and rising, fills the silence. They rise up through the atmosphere. She lies there, eyes open, lost in memories—faces of team members long gone, colleagues who never lived to see the finish line.

Then—

KNOCK. KNOCK.

She doesn't need to ask who it is. "What do you want?" she calls through the door.

"Open up," Lester's voice replies—urgent, breathless.

She drags herself up and opens the door. Lester is standing there, drenched in sweat, eyes wide with anxious energy.

"What's wrong with you?" she asks, brows furrowed.

"We missed something. Something big."

Tericia stiffens. "What?"

"I ran another check. We didn't bring enough Xomithrine. The reaction won't complete in time—look." He thrusts the tablet toward her.

She snatches it, eyes scanning fast. Her heart begins to pound.

"How?" she mutters, pacing now, fingers flicking across the display.

The ship vibrates—then silence. The pressure shift is unmistakable. They are in low orbit.

"No. No, no, no!" Tericia spins around. "We have to stop!"

She bolts down the corridor, racing toward the bridge. Lester follows, tablet in hand.

She throws the door open. "Stop the ship! We need more Xomithrine!"

The vessel shakes, as the main thrusters take over.

"Can't," Captain Roth replies, voice flat. "Best I can do is turn around in a few hours. But that'd mean my job."

"This entire trip will be wasted if you don't," Tericia cries. "We don't have even a tenth of the Xomithrine that we need. Fucking decimal points!"

"Porter," Roth calls out, "check if any outer stations have this Xomithrine shit."

Porter's fingers fly across his console. The silence feels like a noose tightening.

"Waiting," Roth growls as the silence stretches beyond a reasonable moment.

Porter glances up. "Negative."

Tericia slams her hand on the console. "Fuck!"

"Can you make more with materials found along the way?" Roth asks, not really interested in the answer.

"No. We need a specialized lab. We just left one. Blame us if you have to. Just turn this ship around."

Roth stares at her for a moment—then rolls his eyes. "Fine."

She exhales hard. Relief cascades through her like a wave.

"Now go," Roth barks. "Sit in your rooms. Figure out what else you forgot, so I don't have to do this again."

Tericia and Lester slip out silently. Back in her quarters, she speaks first.

"Was that the only issue? I'm not sure we'll survive another mistake."

"I triple-checked the new calculations before I came to you," Lester replies, voice firm.

"Well, we've got a few hours. Let's make sure." She swipes the data to her own device, syncing them up.

They land back at the lab under armed escort—two hired lackeys trailing behind them, weapons drawn. Their presence feels more for intimidation than protection.

Tericia and Lester don't slow down. They storm into the lab and grab every container of Xomithrine they can find, then sweep the shelves for anything that might even remotely be useful.

"Double the Xomithrine—fuck it, triple it, quadruple it," Lester says, voice manic.

"Grab all of it," Tericia orders. "We'll probably run the experiment more than once." Then she whispers to herself, "if we survive the first attempt."

Lester runs for a cart, the lackeys shadowing him, looking confused by the science unfolding around them. They don't understand a word of it. They just watch.

Loaded with materials, they push the cart back toward the ship.

Then the temperature in the corridor drops—not literally, but perceptibly. A presence descends like a shadow.

Tems.

He emerges from the shadows of the ship's ramp, moving with deliberate calm. Every step radiates cold authority. His frame is lean but powerful, like a blade in human form. His eyes—pale, ice-sharp—cut through Tericia and Lester the moment he sees them. There's something in his stare that makes people flinch without knowing why.

"How are my best two scientists today?" Tems asks, his voice low and insincere.

"In a hurry," Tericia replies. "So if you don't mind—"

"Oh, but I do mind," Tems says, stepping forward. "You came back. After wasting more time and money."

There's venom in his tone, controlled but seething. His angular face is carved with precision—cheekbones sharp, jaw locked tight. His black suit fits him like a second skin, every detail pristine.

"It's bad enough we have had to wait a decade. Bad enough we've spent 8.43 trillion credits on this ghost-chasing experiment. And now—"

"We get it," Tericia snaps, cutting him off.

In a flash, Tems closes the distance. He grabs her face with a gloved hand—tight, unyielding.

"Don't ever fucking interrupt me," he hisses, jaw tight, eyes locked on hers with a stare that drills into bone.

Tericia tries to nod, restrained by his grip. Her body stiffens, but she doesn't break.

Lester just stands there, eyes averted, shoulders rigid. Conflict has never been his arena.

Tems lets go with a shove. "Get back on that ship and prove your miracle. Or don't. Either way, I'm done with you."

Tericia and Lester don't reply. They haul the cart up the ramp.

Inside, just past the corridor, Grundle and Stan are dragging a body—Captain Roth—from the bridge.

The door opens just long enough to toss him out like garbage. Before the corpse hits the ground, the hatch begins to close.

Tericia stares as they roll the cart past, her jaw clenched.

"These next six weeks are going to suck," Lester whispers.

Tericia just nods, her eyes still locked on the spot where Roth's body disappeared.

CHAPTER 3

"You fuck with me or put my life at risk," Earl growls, his breath hot and sour as he leans inches from Lester's face, "you'll find yourself on a long, cold walk through the vacuum of space."

Lester doesn't flinch, but his throat tightens. Earl's words aren't bluster—they're a promise.

"It wasn't his fault," Tericia says quickly, standing from her seated position. "The pressure we're under—it makes us miss—"

"I DON'T FUCKING CARE!" Earl's voice explodes across the room as he whips toward her. His face is flushed with rage, his eyes wild. He lunges close, so close she can feel the heat off his skin. "I've got one job. And screwing that up means my death. You saw what happened when he turned back. That shit's not happening again. If you forgot anything else, I swear you won't "realize it" until we're at the drop point and your experiment fails—and then it'll be your death, not mine. AM I FUCKING CLEAR!?"

Tericia doesn't blink. She nods. So does Lester, slower, more reluctant.

Earl straightens, rolling his neck like he's readying for a fight that never came.

"Bugs and Meat will be watching your every move," he adds, jerking a thumb toward the two shadows lingering in the doorway. The names suit them. Bugs is thin, wiry, eyes twitching constantly like he's waiting for a threat that never arrives. Meat is pure bulk, all neck and shoulders, with dead, flat eyes that don't blink nearly enough.

"You won't even be able to take a shit without them sifting through it after," Earl says, grinning now—a grin too wide, too pleased with itself, like a kid who just got away with kicking someone down the stairs.

Tericia keeps her voice level. "Will there be anything else?" She's asks, already turning away before he can respond, her tone making it clear: this conversation is over.

But Earl's hand shoots out. He grabs her arm, spins her around, and slams her against the metal wall hard enough to rattle the paneling.

"You can't kill us," she says evenly, her voice unshaken. "You're under strict orders to deliver us alive. Otherwise, it'll be your corpse they find floating out here."

Earl seethes, jaw flexing, but the truth of her words chains him down. He throws her to the side, spitting out his anger as he storms from the room.

Lester moves to Tericia immediately. "Are you okay?" he asks, his voice low.

"Sure," she mutters, brushing herself off. "Except for these two fuckers."

She gestures to Bugs and Meat, who simply stare back in silence. There's no reaction. No blink. Just presence. Watching.

"I'm going to bed," Lester says. "Had enough fun for one day. Wake me up when we're six weeks older."

"If only," Tericia sighs. She pulls him into a quick, tight hug.

Then, close to his ear, she whispers, "I have a plan."

Lester stiffens slightly, not daring to react with Bugs and Meat still watching. He wants to respond—something subtle, something safe—but his mouth betrays him before his brain can catch up.

"Love you too."

They both freeze. Tericia pulls back. Her brows rise slightly in confusion. Lester's face goes pale.

They stare at each other.

Lester looks like he wants to crawl out of his own skin. Tericia doesn't move, doesn't speak—just watches him.

Then, without another word, they part. Lester heads toward his quarters, walking too quickly. Tericia lingers, eyes on his back as he disappears. Bugs and Meat follow—Bugs sticking to Tericia, Meat shadowing Lester.

Tericia enters her room, Bugs trailing behind. As she tries to close the door, he steps forward.

"Excuse me?" she snaps, placing a firm hand against the frame. "Where the fuck do you think you're going?"

Bugs raises a brow and motions to the interior of her quarters.

"Yeah, no. You're not watching me change, or sleep, or piss. I'm not your prisoner. I'm not a damn zoo animal. You wait out here. Got it?"

She slams the door in his face and twists the lock.

She exhales hard, then peels off her work clothes and changes into worn pajamas—soft fabric, old and frayed at the cuffs. She brews tea using the auto-dispenser, sits down at the small table, and begins scrolling through data, forcing her brain to focus.

Then—CRASH.

The door bursts open.

Tericia jolts up as Earl storms in, dragging Bugs by the collar.

"Did I not make myself clear!?" he shouts, hurling Bugs to the ground like a sack of meat. "This man is to watch. Your. Every! Move!" Each of Earl's words louder and more intense than the previous one.

Tericia stands her ground. Calm. Unshaken.

"Earl, go fuck yourself," she says evenly. "I told Bugs I'm not your prisoner. I'm not here for your entertainment. You wouldn't even have this job if it weren't for us. So take your little boy-toy and crawl back into whatever vent you slithered out of."

Earl's face darkens. "You little bitch," he hisses, lunging forward.

"I wouldn't," Tericia says, her voice barely above a whisper—but every syllable lands like a gunshot.

He pauses—hesitates—just long enough.

That's all she needs.

Her hand slams down on the small device next to her tea. From above, a thick, reinforced bar drops from a ceiling compartment and cracks Earl squarely in the skull.

Electricity pulses through it, sending him into full-body convulsions. He drops to the floor, seizing uncontrollably.

Bugs jumps back, panic flickering across his face. He looks up. Left. Right. Calculating his odds of getting to Tericia.

"Do you really want to test your luck, Bugs?" Tericia asks, folding her arms and crossing one leg over the other, leaning back in the chair, showing an edge of confidence.

He freezes.

"Drag your boss out of here. Then tell Meat to back off Lester."

Still frozen.

"Which word didn't you understand?" Her tone sharpens like a scalpel, her eyes finally meeting his.

Bugs fumbles with his weapon—then slowly holsters it. He grabs Earl's limp wrists and begins dragging him toward the door.

Tericia follows. Just before the door closes, she offers Bugs a bright, unbothered smile.

"Next six weeks might not suck after all," she says, turning back inside.

She sips her tea slowly, savoring it. Then she heads to bed and stretches out under the thin blankets. Her eyes close, but her thoughts remain loud.

Lester said he loves me.

She doesn't know what to do with that.

But for tonight, she lets herself smile.

CHAPTER 4

"We're here," Earl calls through Tericia's door, his tone flat.

"Fuck off!" Tericia shouts, out of breath.

"I love it when you talk dirty," Lester adds, also panting.

"Fuck you," she says, smiling as she leans in and kisses him again.

Their bodies are tangled under thin sheets, warm from exertion, the tension of the last six weeks finally melting into something more human—more intimate.

After a few more minutes, Tericia rolls onto her back and exhales. "I guess we should go to work."

Lester groans. "I guess so."

They climb out of bed, tossing on lab suits with the fluid ease of people who've done this a thousand times. They gather their gear and head for the cargo bay.

"These six weeks flew by," Lester says, their footsteps echoing along the narrow corridor.

"Yeah," Tericia says, slipping her hand into his. "Once we put the crew in their place and figured *this* out, it almost felt... normal." Her eyes drifting to his hand and then to his eyes.

They arrive at the cargo bay. In the center, a large cube rests in place—sealed tight, two meters to a side. The containment unit hums faintly. Inside waits the culmination of a decade's worth of theory, failure, betrayal, and breakthroughs. Corporate security protocols had ensured they couldn't touch the device in transit, out of fear of sabotage.

Now, finally, it's time.

While the final seal counts down, they prep everything else. Carts roll out, tools clatter into trays, tanks of fuel standing ready until they're secured into place.

Then—

Breep. Breep. Breep.

A warning to move out of the way.

A sharp hiss follows, the pressurized seal breaking. The cube unlocks with a gentle release of air, like the project itself taking its first breath.

"Earl. Bugs. Meat," Tericia calls out, motioning. "Help move those panels so we can reach the device."

The men comply without a word. No sass, no pushback. Their fear of Tericia has become a quiet, well-earned respect.

Tericia and Lester step in, their hands moving across the machine's sleek surface with surgical precision. They attach the fuel cells, check seals, run diagnostics, tighten bolts, and unlock display panels. The screen lights up and begins a checklist.

Structural integrity… OK. Power routing… OK. Xomithrine load… OK.

Then a flicker.

Critical error: Node 11.

"Lester," Tericia says without even looking. "Node 11 again."

"I hate that node. I don't know why it always fails," but the gulp in his throat might be his only tell. He knows what node 11 is and what it does.

"It doesn't matter. Remove it for now. Replace it with this," Tericia says, handing a replacement part to Lester.

He groans and heads over, prying open a panel and swapping out the component with practiced ease. A twist of a knob. A flick of a lever.

"All set," he says, coming back to the controls of the machine.

The screen turns green across the board. All systems: go.

With one final switch, the device slides gently across the floor on its microslide footers, hovering like it's weightless. The footers hum beneath it—smooth, frictionless when they need to be, locked down when they don't. They guide it toward the bay doors and fix it in place.

Then come the **PortaPrellant Pro** units—cube-shaped propulsion devices, each with three directional ports. Lester snaps them into place at each corner of the machine. The cubes' syncing system aligns the device in the vacuum of space with near-microscopic precision.

Tericia steps away from the machine and climbs into the observation room overlooking the cargo bay.

She grabs and presses the mic button. "You all might want to clear out. We're opening the door."

Everyone scatters out of the cargo bay and joins her, watching from behind the glass.

She taps the START button.

A klaxon sounds. The bay depressurizes. The doors yaw open, revealing the blackness of deep space—pure and vast, beyond the Oort Cloud, beyond gravity's leash.

The machine slides forward, drifting slowly into open space. Lester's hands move over his controls, nudging it to a precise distance.

"Are we at a safe range?" Earl asks, crossing his arms.

"Doesn't matter," Tericia says without looking at him. "Either we're safe or we're dead. The only way we were ever going to test this, to make sure it works, was out here. Away from our sun's gravity. If we are wrong in our calculations and we did this back home, well... Earth wouldn't exist anymore. So, yeah. We are at a safe range from Earth."

Earl gulps his fear away. Tericia doesn't see it, but she knows she struck a cord.

She taps the screen again to begin the sequence.

A countdown begins to roll.

Ten.

Tericia's chest rises with each breath. Ten years. Every failure. Every late night. Every betrayal.

Nine.

Lester watches her more than the screen.

Eight.

Earl doesn't move. His distrust is visible in every stiff inch of his posture.

Seven.

Tericia's smile grows, her fingers tightening around the edge of the console.

Six.

Lester crosses his fingers without realizing.

Five.

She does too.

Four.

No one speaks. No one breathes.

Three.

Her eyes lock on the display—unblinking.

Two.

Lester leans closer, triple-checking readings.

One.

"Execute!" Tericia shouts.

The machine erupts to life.

A brilliant violet laser fires into the void. Then a second reaction—a glowing blue spiral forms around the laser's path. It spins, clockwise, chasing the beam. A third pulse surges from the Xomithrine core—a beam of energy unlike anything seen before.

A blackness forms. Dense. Not empty—but full, like the absence of everything familiar. It blooms into a massive spiral, surrounded by swirling blue energy. The shape of space itself begins to bend.

Stars beyond it shift—new stars, distorted and strange, as though seen through water until it finally shifts to a clear view of the stars beyond.

Tericia slams the halt sequence, and the beams dissipate. But the anomaly remains.

A perfect, spiraling gateway. Still. Open.

"Holy shit!" Tericia cries. She grabs Lester's hands and jumps up and down like a child seeing snow for the first time. "We did it!"

"It's stable too!" Lester says, his voice cracking with joy.

Earl, still unimpressed, squints at the window. "Great. What is it?"

Tericia turns to him slowly, still smiling. "You mean... they sent you out here to babysit us, and you don't even know what you were guarding?"

"They don't tell me anything. Just where to fly."

She laughs and walks back to the console, face glowing. "Earl," she says, "you are witnessing the first man-made wormhole. We built Holepunch here to literally punch holes in space. This wormhole device is the first of its kind."

Earl raises an eyebrow. "Oh."

Then he sits down and starts swiping through a tablet like she just told him the microwave beeped.

Tericia shakes her head, bemused. "Sending a probe," she mutters, then turns back to her instruments.

Lester runs the sequence. "Probe approaching the wormhole in three... two... one..."

The probe slips into the event field and disappears briefly. The gateway ripples gently, like a pond disturbed by a single stone, but only for a few seconds. Then, they see the probe on the other side of the swirling wonder.

"Where does it go?" Earl asks, finally showing an ounce of curiosity.

"No idea," Tericia replies. "The first goal was just to see if we could make it. The next step is to see if it is repeatable. The final step is controlling where it goes."

"Seems pointless if you can't pick your destination," Earl says with a huff.

"Science is a slow process," Tericia says, all too happy to be offended.

"Receiving probe data," Lester announces, his giddiness continues. "Direct line of sight works from wherever this wormhole leads."

Tericia spins toward him, breath caught in her throat.

The data comes in—an avalanche of information, numbers, radiation patterns, spatial telemetry—but no immediate answer.

"This is going to take a while to sort through," Lester says.

"I'm okay with that," Tericia replies, eyes never leaving the screen. "In the meantime… I'll let Tems know it was a success."

CHAPTER 5

"Figure it out. Now!" Tems yells, his voice slicing through the comms, one last command before the screen goes black.

"Fuck you too," Tericia mutters, alone now with the echo of her rage.

She exhales hard and lets her forehead rest against the cold metal wall of the comm station. Talking to Tems is like trying to hold a conversation while your head is inside a meat grinder. Every exchange leaves you bruised.

'I swear that man doesn't sleep. Doesn't eat. Just stalks us like a malfunctioning AI with anger issues,' she thinks.

Her boots clunk softly down the hall as she heads towards Lester's quarters. She's still muttering to herself, too drained to filter her thoughts. "Oh, we're figuring it out, all right, you sadistic fuck. Would've figured it out anyway. No need to bark threats like we're your attack dogs. We built this. It's our baby. You're just squatting on top of it. Suffocating any life out of it you can."

"What was that?" Lester asks, stepping into the hall just in time to catch the tail end of her rant.

Tericia straightens. "Nothing. Just reliving another lovely conversation with Tems."

"Let me guess—'figure it out,' 'do more,' and my favorite: 'yesterday.'"

"Bingo. He practically screamed it through the screen. And now I'm stuck hearing his voice echoing around my skull like a broken alarm."

"You okay?" Lester asks, hoping to find some way to console her.

Tericia shrugs. "Doesn't matter. What matters is this wormhole. Got any updates?"

Lester nods, already scrolling through data on his tablet. "We know we can go back and forth. And it's held for…" he glances at the timer on his wrist, "…two hundred and eighteen minutes. Still stable."

Tericia's shoulders drop a little. Relief and pride mixing in her chest. "That's… significant."

"Yeah. But now we need to figure out what happens when it closes. Can we reopen to the same location? That's the big one."

"We have a whole list: how long do they last, can we extend the duration, scale the size, can we lock onto coordinates from anywhere…" Tericia sighs. "And according to Tems, we needed all that yesterday."

"Fuck that guy." Lester tilts her chin up gently, forcing eye contact. His thumb brushes across her jaw. "We'll get there. He can scream into the void for all I care."

She smiles, eyes softening. "Thanks."

He leans down and kisses her—quiet, grounding.

"Let's figure something out," she says, stepping back with a grin, "and then I'll take you back to my quarters to share something new."

Lester's grin widens. "I'm in."

They head toward the lab station when—

BEEP. BEEP. BEEP.

Holepunch's notification system blares. Lester rushes forward.

"Star mapping complete!" he says, practically bouncing. "We have the coordinates!"

Tericia moves beside him, scanning the readout. Her breath catches.

"A binary star system," Lester says. "5,911 light-years from Earth. Still in our galaxy."

They both stare at the screen, then at each other. Elation builds. It's real.

Then—FLASH.

A sudden pulse of light from the wormhole. A shimmer across the black.

They whip their heads toward the viewport.

Another flash. Then another. Closer together.

And then—flicker. A smaller flicker than the large flashes. Collapse.

The wormhole blinks out of existence as if it never was.

A silence follows. Not of peace—but of consequence.

"That was fast," Lester says. "No warning window. You see a flash? You're too late."

Tericia exhales slowly. "Well. At least we know the window now. Roughly three and a half hours. Give or take."

Lester nods. "Want to try again? See if we can hit the same coordinates?"

"Let's do it."

They move quickly, repeating their steps with calm precision—same parameters, same inputs, same numbers. Holepunch hums back to life. The space outside bends, and once again, a swirling black spiral opens.

Lester watches intently. "I can't tell."

"Don't guess," Tericia says, firm. "Send a probe."

He launches it. It slides across space and slips into the wormhole with the same clean entry.

They wait in silence.

Lester paces slightly. "Now that we know what to look for, verifying the location shouldn't take long."

"Why are you explaining this to me like I don't already know it?" Tericia asks, arching a brow.

"Because I'm excited. And maybe paranoid. I've always figured someone's listening in."

Tericia rolls her eyes. "You think Tems has someone planted in the oxygen tanks?"

"Wouldn't surprise me."

Tericia rolls her eyes. It wouldn't surprise her either.

Minutes pass.

Then—DING.

"Same coordinates," Lester says, barely containing himself. "It's the same exact location!"

"Holy shit..." Tericia whispers. "Repeatable. That means..."

"We did it!" Lester laughs. "This isn't just theory anymore."

"We did something," Tericia says, though a smile tugs at her lips. "We still need to test if the wormhole can be reopened to the same point from another location."

"Like dialing coordinates from anywhere in the universe," Lester says. "Intergalactic GPS."

"Exactly. We still don't know if distance breaks the link."

Lester pulls up another screen, already prepping the next calibration.

"Let's head home," Tericia says. "We've proved it's safe. We didn't evaporate into the void, there was no gravitational implosion. Earth won't turn into a black hole. Life won't get sucked into a single point. That should count for something."

He nods. "We've earned the return trip."

"I'll go tell the captain," Tericia says, already heading out, her mind swimming with plans—and new possibilities.

CHAPTER 6

"I think you forget how hard it was just to build the prototype!" Tericia shouts into the screen, pacing. Her hair clings to her face with sweat, and her voice trembles—not from fear, but from sheer exhaustion. "You're demanding we figure out how to aim a wormhole across the galaxy like it's a casual request. That could take another ten years!"

"The fuck it will!" Tems growls back, his face crackling across the display. His evil eyes lock onto hers like weapons. "You'll figure it out by year's end, or I'll replace you with someone who can."

"I've been asking for help—a team, more eyes, support! Not to be replaced. Why won't you—"

"Just fucking make it happen, or reality won't be pretty for you," Tems threatens. "And start the fucking test!"

"We don't have enough—"

"I DON'T FUCKING CARE! SEND SOMEONE!"

The feed cuts to black.

Tericia stands motionless in the cold silence, breath ragged. Her face is flushed with anger, but her body slumps with defeat.

She doesn't hear Lester approach until he's next to her, limping slightly as he carries two canisters of water. His cheek is bruised, his steps stiff from another beating.

Tericia turns. And breaks.

Tears fall, unguarded, and Lester is there immediately, pulling her into his arms.

"It's going to be okay," he whispers. "We'll figure it out."

"Or we die," she says into his shoulder.

"They can't afford to kill us. They might threaten it—but they'd be back to square one without us. I made sure of that. As you know."

Tericia looks up at him, her face streaked with tears. "Even with all that... I can't think straight anymore. I'm starving, bruised, barely sleeping."

"I know." Lester brushes her hair back, softly. "We're prisoners. Tortured. Starved. Beaten. And we're expected to solve something the universe itself barely understands."

He presses his forehead to hers. "But we're still here. And we're still together."

Tericia closes her eyes and just holds him.

The observation room buzzes with quiet tension. A small single-pilot ship floats in front of the wormhole's edge— sleek, black, and armed with sensors.

Inside it, sits Parmen.

A former fighter pilot who still looks like he just stepped off a recruitment poster. Cocky and confident, muscles tight under his flight suit, his dark hair styled like he still has a regulation to follow. Every inch of him screams control and charm. The kind of man who grins in the face of death just to see if it flinches.

"He volunteered for this," Lester mutters softly, shaking his head.

He volunteered to be the first human to go through a wormhole. Sure, probes have been sent back and forth for months now, but never a human.

Tems wants this to happen. So, it is happening, despite Tericia's desperate attempts to have other organic material go through first.

"Ready?" Tericia asks over comms, keeping her tone neutral, despite the knot in her gut.

"Ready!" Parmen answers with a grin they can feel through the speakers. "Crossing the barrier in ten seconds."

Tericia keeps her hands folded tightly behind her back. Lester leans closer to the screen, eyes wide with hope— and worry.

"Going through now," Parmen says.

The ship glides forward, and just like the probes before it, vanishes into the shimmering mouth of the wormhole.

Seconds later, his voice returns as does the image of his ship. "Looks the same. Didn't feel a thing. Not even a bump."

Lester exhales, grinning. "It worked."

"Come on back," Tericia says. "That was the test."

Parmen's ship slips back through, emerging like a head poking out from under the water's surface but without the splashing. The ship returns unscathed. No smoke. No damage. No anomalies.

"You just became the first person in human history to travel through a man-made wormhole," Lester says. "And the first human to be in the presence of a new star system."

"I'll inform Tems," Tericia mutters, turning from the screen. Her voice is dull. Not from lack of pride—but from the knowledge that it won't be enough.

It never is.

Weeks pass, the tests continue, but still no satisfactory result that puts Tems at ease.

The station orbits the Moon in cold, endless silence. Time blurs into darkness and hunger. Beatings are routine. Rations earned only when progress is made.

They work until their hands tremble from dehydration. Sleep comes only in shallow hours.

The wormhole pulses outside like a heart, a hole in space tethered by hope and fear.

Then—

"Hello?"

A voice. Young. Curious. Too loud.

Lester juts up and heads into the cargo bay. He rounds the corner and sees a young man standing there. Lester quickly looks around wondering why the jailers aren't here. 'Probably drunk and asleep, like usual,' Lester says to himself.

Tericia walks in next and freezes when she sees him.

"Are you here to kill us?" she asks, half-hopeful, half-horrified.

"Kill you?" The man asks. "What? Why? No! I'm here to help with the project."

Tericia looks at Lester as he looks back at her. They both look with confusion in their eyes, then simultaneously look back to this new person.

"And you are?" Lester asks.

"Nick, well, Nicholas, but I go by Nick."

"Nick. Hmmm…do you know why you are here? Who sent you? What you signed up for?" Tericia asks.

"All I know is that I was approached by Harry Telber at Borvil and asked if I would be interested in working on the newest and most amazing scientific…"

"So, you don't have a clue. If you can turn back now, do. Trust me." Tericia snaps. "Don't learn about this place if you can still leave."

Nick looks worried and then looks back toward the airlock. All three of them see the transport leave.

Lester stares at him, then back at the sealed transport ship, now already drifting away.

Tericia curses under her breath. "Too late now."

"Wait," Nick says, his smile faltering. "Why? What's going on?"

"Fuck," Tericia says in a low tone of pity. "I guess, welcome. Welcome to wormholes 101 and our inability to do what Tems wants. If you can't figure it out, well, let me

just ask bluntly—have you ever experienced torture?"
Tericia asks in defeat.

Nick's expression collapses into a mixture of panic and
disbelief. He starts to sweat, eyes darting around the cargo
bay like he's only just realized how claustrophobic it really
is.

"Did you say... torture?" he asks weakly.

"And wormholes," Lester adds, deadpan.

"Can't tell if you're excited or terrified," Lester continues,
raising an eyebrow.

Nick doesn't answer. Just stands frozen.

"Come on," Tericia says. "We'll get you settled before
Dweeb and Doofus wake up from their nightly binge."

CHAPTER 7

A few weeks later, in a rare break from the chaos, Tericia, Lester, and Nick sit together in the galley.

It's quiet—too quiet for the weight this project carries. But right now, it's food that matters. Real food. After months of deprivation, the three had finally convinced their captors that starving your geniuses wasn't exactly a productivity booster.

Science won one battle. Just one.

Nick pokes at his food, eyes darting between the others. His boyish face is drawn tight with fatigue, but his eyes—still bright—flicker with something else: hope... and frustration.

"You guys," Nick says, chewing slowly on the idea forming in his head while also chewing on some food. "Have you tried changing the two focal points?"

Lester doesn't look up. "They're fixed in place," he mumbles through a mouthful of food.

"Our calculations—" Tericia begins.

"Our calculations," Nick interrupts sharply. "God, I'm tired of hearing that. I wasn't brought here to hear you recite why nothing can change. You proved the fucking science. Now tweak it. Try shit. Fail forward."

His voice echoes in the room, sharp enough to pierce the fatigue hanging over them.

Tericia and Lester exchange a glance. A heavy one. Nick isn't wrong.

Lester clears his throat. "Sorry, Nick. Go on. What are you thinking?"

Nick hesitates. "Are you actually going to listen, or are we going to do the usual 'thanks but no thanks' thing?"

Tericia softens, but her voice stays grounded. "Nick, listen… We've been working on this thing for over a decade. We could find every control of Holepunch blindfolded. We can recite the code like a bible thumper can recite passages. It's not that we don't respect your ideas. It's just—most of them are things we've already asked ourselves. Already tried. Already did the calcul…" And she stops herself before finishing the word.

"Then let me ask them again," Nick replies. "That's how I work through things. Sometimes asking the question out loud helps me find the answer."

"Fair," Lester says, still chewing. "So, talk."

Nick sits straighter, his fear momentarily drowned by focus. He looks younger than anyone in the room, yet there's something older in his tone now—like someone who's aged too fast under pressure.

"It probably wouldn't take more than a few microns of change," he says slowly, "but adjusting the distance between the two focal points could expand or contract the wormhole. We treat focal points as static, but wormholes are fourth-dimensional. So maybe it's not about shifting position—it's about shifting size. Change the spacing, change the shape."

Lester blinks.

Tericia sets down her fork.

"There was almost nothing about that sentence that made sense," she says. Then smiles. "But fuck it. Worth a shot. We'd need an adjustable interface. Right now, the focal point is locked."

Nick bites into a bit of bread and suppresses a grin. For the first time, he's been heard.

Weeks later, the team stands around a console, fatigue forgotten for the moment. The station hums with tension.

"Calibration testing complete," Tericia says, stepping back. "I guess it's time to test your hypothesis."

"Firing up the device," Lester confirms.

They've moved Holepunch inside the station now—no longer afraid it'll explode or bend gravity in ways that collapse everything nearby. The calculations had predicted worst-case scenarios that never came. So now? It's about pushing the boundaries.

"Start with the current setting," Nick says, practically vibrating with anticipation. "Then move the focal point before cutting the fuel."

The wormhole ignites—violet light twisting into space just like it has countless times.

"Adjusting," Lester says, fingers turning a new knob, each adjust moving the focal points in such small increments that it would take a microscope to see the change.

"Wormhole decreasing in size!" Tericia calls, watching the data stream. "It's actually working!"

"Try turning it the other way. Try increasing it!" Nick shouts, excitement overtaking his tone.

Lester adjusts the controls the other direction.

"It's growing!" Tericia says, her voice cracking with awe. "Nick!"

"I know! It's awesome!" Nick's smile threatens to crack his face in half.

They keep pushing, watching the wormhole stretch wider and wider. The readout shows they're nearing the limits of the containment frame.

"That's large enough for any known ship," Tericia says breathlessly.

She presses the termination protocol. The beams shut off. The wormhole remains.

"This is so cool," Nick whispers, eyes wide.

But the celebration is short-lived.

FLASH.

Then another.

And another.

The wormhole flickers rapidly—then collapses in on itself.

"What?!" Lester shouts.

Nick frowns. "Maybe the larger the aperture, the shorter the window. Makes sense—it's more unstable."

Tericia nods slowly. "Still… we needed to know. And know that we know, I have to tell Tems. And of course, Tems is going to demand more."

"Yeah," Lester says. "Next he'll want it big, stable, reusable, and—oh right— even more portable than it already is."

"Send someone through. Open it from the other side," Tericia mutters darkly. "Shit. We'll have to build a second device. See if two can sync. One to go through, one to come back."

"Not it," Lester says quickly, raising both hands.

Nick and Tericia blink at him.

"I'm not telling Tems we need a second one," Lester says. "I'd rather eject myself into space."

"I'll do it," Tericia sighs. "I'm used to his bullshit."

"Say that again?" Tericia asks, eyes narrowing at the screen.

"Why the fuck wouldn't we?!" Tems snarls. "WE. DON'T. TAKE. CHANCES."

His glare could shatter steel. His jaw is clenched like he's chewing rocks.

"Where is it? When can you get it here?" Tericia presses.

Tems sneers. "You think we'd put both devices in the same place at the same time? Use what you have. You run your test up there. We run ours down here."

"But we haven't tested—"

"Test what fucking matters!" Tems roars. "If your guy doesn't come back, then maybe we will talk. Until then— GET TO FUCKING WORK!"

The screen cuts out. As always, Tems never lets anyone else have the last word.

"Fucker," Tericia growls, then spins around and storms out of the room.

Time to send Parmen to his possible death. Or worse, to be lost in space forever.

CHAPTER 8

"I've got it!" Parmen barks, throwing up a hand. "You've shown me twenty-six times. I've been watching you open this thing for months. I know how it works."

Tericia opens her mouth.

"We just want to make sure—"

"That I can handle any problems," Parmen snaps, cutting Lester off. "Yes, you've said that. Repeatedly. You say it like I'm a deaf child with a toy spaceship. I'm good."

His confidence hits the room like pressure from a sealed bulkhead. Sharp jaw, flight suit tight over lean muscle, posture locked. Parmen still moves like a decorated military man—even if he's been running ops for corporations lately. To him, this isn't danger. It's legacy.

Lester, Tericia, and Nick drop their gazes. The man isn't wrong.

"What are you really worried about?" Parmen asks, voice cooling. "You think I'm afraid of dying? I signed up knowing the odds. There's something else bothering you."

"That's not your concern," Tericia says tightly. "Dead or alive, the outcome is the same for us. Now get going."

That silences the room. Lester, Nick and Parmen all stare at Tericia. Her words hanging in the air, waiting to be exposed.

Parmen frowns. "What does that mean?"

Tericia steps closer to the viewport, voice flat. "Once this technology allows people to jump across the galaxy freely, Borvil wins. They'll control all space travel. Trade. Migration. Exploration. Everything. They'll own the stars. Hell, they'll own travel in and around Earth itself. Their leadership will take over. Anything they want will be theirs. Everyone who wants in will bow to them. They will become dictators, defining their own way forward."

She turns, her expression hard. "You've seen what Tems is like. Imagine an entire fleet of Tems's controlling colonies, ports, entire planets. That's the world we're building. That's the world we give them if we succeed."

The silence is heavier now. The realization, palpable. The truth, spoken.

Lester finally breaks the silence. "They said the second device was built exactly the same, right?"

"Yes," Tericia answers, a confused look etched while she looks at Lester for answers.

"Good," Lester says, nodding slowly.

"Why?" she asks.

"I'll explain later. But that's a very good thing."

"This is great and all," Parmen says, stretching, "but I've got a test to run. We don't have a galaxy to save today. Just a pilot to strand."

He heads out of the room and toward the docking bay without waiting for permission, climbing into his ship.

The team watches as the vessel detaches from the station. Attached to the hull is the wormhole generator—streamlined, compact, and humming with power.

"Calibrating aperture for my ship," Parmen calls over comms.

Tericia, Lester, and Nick monitor the data in real time. Everything checks out.

The wormhole opens, just wide enough to accommodate the small ship.

Parmen flies through as he has many times before.

But instead of turning back, he keeps going—thousands of meters forward, then stops and turns. He waits. Watching.

"Just stay where you are," Tericia says, repeating instructions for the umpteenth time. "If the Holepunch doesn't open a return trip, don't go through. Just …"

The wormhole flickers.

Then vanishes.

"…stay put."

Parmen had pressed the newly installed and tested abort feature. It closes the wormhole without having to wait for it to close on its own.

Nick found a way to close it. Tericia and Lester never looked for that option. But being able to close the wormhole at will seemed important after they realized they could.

"It's been too long," Nick says, pacing behind them.

"Yes. We know," Lester and Tericia reply in unison.

"I've already contacted Tems," Tericia adds. "Told him we need the second device to bring Parmen back. If it's a true duplicate, we can align the signals and reopen the exact same location."

Nick scoffs. "You two talk like tour guides. You know we know this, right?"

"It's how we cope," Lester says with a faint smile. "We repeat the plan to reassure ourselves. Repetition helps us stay grounded."

Tericia nods. "And yeah. It's probably annoying."

Nick rolls his eyes. "You guys have been together too long."

"You all should get some rest," Tericia suggests. "We have to wait a few hours for someone to bring up the second device. Maybe even days. We might as well get rest while we can."

Lester claps Nick on the back as he walks by. "That means you too."

"And you," he adds to Tericia, with a wink.

Tericia smiles faintly and follows him out.

BEEP BEEP BEEP.

The proximity alarm jolts them awake and tells them that someone is approaching the station.

They rush to the observation room in time to see a ship descending into the bay. A cargo hauler. A containment lift behind it. The second wormhole generator appearing from its hull.

But more than that—Tems.

He marches from the ship like a weapon given legs. Adjusting his tie. Cracking his neck side to side. His stare burns cold as ever.

Tericia and Lester instinctively tense as the device is offloaded behind him.

Tems enters the observation deck with calculated slowness.

"So," he begins, voice full of acid, "you fucked up the test. We've now got a man stranded five thousand light-years from Earth. Stellar work."

He walks past them, inspecting each of their faces like a drill sergeant deciding who to punish first.

"I should shoot one of you," he says casually. "But I can't decide who. Maybe I'll let you choose," he says, looking at Tericia in the eyes.

He sits. Crosses his legs and proceeds to eyeball each member of the crew.

"You can't be serious," Tericia says.

Tems simply raises his eyebrows. "Waiting."

"You know what? No," Tericia says, straightening. "We're not playing your game. We'll bring Parmen back. We have your second device. We move forward."

Tems rises. Slowly.

He walks to her. Inches from her face.

"Maybe I should kill you for your defiance," he says, barely moving his mouth.

He turns to Lester. "Or you. Just to teach her a lesson."

Then finally to Nick.

"Or the new kid. You've been here for weeks and contributed nothing I've asked for."

Something in his voice shifts—like he knows more than he should. Tericia catches it. A whisper of suspicion.

"You didn't bring him here for us, did you?" she asks softly.

Nick stiffens. Tems ignores her as he sits again, waiting for a decision to be made.

"Just leave us alone," she says louder. "We're working. We're making progress."

Nick steps forward. "I've been working on a targeting algorithm. I'm close. I'm just not allowed to share ideas until I have proof."

"That's not what we meant," Lester says, his disappointment sharp.

Nick's mask cracks. "Whatever. I have ideas. You just suck at listening."

Tems claps his hands slowly, three times. "This is fun. First time I've seen you argue. Very enlightening."

He steps toward the window as the second device is hauled into place.

"Now shut your fucking mouths and listen closely. The second device is being moved into position. You will get Parmen back. Either today, or whenever you figure out a location specific solution. But he isn't your biggest concern. You have one more month to figure it all out. Or, you will be joining Parmen in a different part of the galaxy. Just without a ship. Get my point!"

He pulls a weapon from his coat, and shoots Lester in the leg.

Lester collapses, screaming.

"Lester!" Tericia cries, rushing to him looking to Tems. "You fucking monster!"

Tems doesn't flinch. He turns his stare to Nick—pointed. Intentional.

It's a message. Do what you were sent to do.

"Next time it won't be his leg, but your head," Tems says calmly, returning his gaze to Tericia, just as he turns to leave the room to get back into his ship.

Then he pauses. The guards that were left at the station to keep an eye on the team—finally stirred by the commotion—enter the room, clearly drunk.

Tems turns, sees the guards, raises his weapon, and executes them both without hesitation. A shot to each of their heads.

"Fucking worthless," he growls.

Tems sees that everyone is watching. He looks at them and smiles as he lets loose a few more rounds into each guard.

Then he sinisterly points his weapon at Tericia and mouths the words, "One month."

He presses the trigger, but it only makes a click.

He has spent all of his rounds on the guards. But has also made his point. Tems doesn't value Tericia's life. He will happily kill her and now Tericia knows it.

Tems finally turns and leaves. His presence has made things more difficult, as it always does. Impossible deadlines left more difficult with the need to clean up after his mess.

CHAPTER 9

"Nick, you have three seconds to explain yourself," Tericia's voice is calm. Too calm.

Nick stands frozen in the cargo transfer airlock, caught in the thin space between the sealed interior and the void of space beyond. One step. One button press. That's all it will take.

"I—I don't know what you want from me!" he stammers, panic blooming in his eyes.

Tericia doesn't blink. "I saw Tems's face. I saw the way he looked at you. He wasn't mad you failed me—he was mad you failed him. That wasn't fear in your eyes, Nick. That was shame. The kind you get when you disappoint a parent. You had the look of failure, something deeper than this project."

She lifts her hand, hovering over the airlock release.

"Two seconds," she says, reminding him that his time is about to be cut short.

Nick's breath catches in his throat. "Seriously—I was just trying to stay alive! I didn't want him to shoot me too!"

"One," she says, her voice colder now.

Nick flinches. "I don't know anything!"

"I guess I'll never know," Tericia replies, pressing her hand down.

"Stop! Stop! Just wait—" Nick gasps, his voice cracking. "I'll talk!"

She keeps her hand hovering.

"He sent me up here for two reasons!" Nick blurts out, his eyes tracking Terica's hand, hoping she will move it from the release button.

"Reason number one?" Tericia asks, still focused on the console.

"Primarily to make sure you succeed. I swear. I am a scientist. I do have ideas. He knew I could help you finish it."

"Number two?" she asks, tone unwavering.

Nick looks down, his tone laced with sadness, "To kill you. Once it's done."

Silence.

"He's got my family," Nick says, choking on the words. "If we don't figure it out by the end of the month, they die. If we do... and I don't kill you... they still die."

Tericia presses a button—the one just below her hand.

"NO!!" Nick shouts, seeing Tericia move her hand.

The inner cargo door hisses open in front of him.

Nick stumbles forward, collapsing to his knees as the tension leaves his body in a single, violent exhale. He trembles. Pale. Silent.

Tericia stares down at him, expression unreadable.

"We'll talk. But first—we check on Lester."

She turns and walks out. Nick doesn't move for several seconds, then stumbles to his feet.

"I—I'll catch up. I need to pee," he says weakly. "Almost didn't make it just now…"

In the medical bay, Tericia sits beside Lester, holding his hand. The automated repair unit continues its work, encasing his wounded leg in biogel while surgical arms operate beneath.

Lester stirs, barely able to open his eyes. "Hey, love."

"You're not supposed to be awake," Tericia says softly.

"Nerve block only works on the leg," he slurs with a lazy smile. "Woke me up to let me know."

"I'm going to fix this," she whispers, clutching his hand tighter.

"The machine is already fixing it," he mumbles, half-conscious, his words slurring like a drunk fresh from the bar.

"Still funny when drugged," she smiles and kisses him gently.

As she pulls back, her eyes flick toward the doorway—Nick has arrived.

Her expression hardens.

She moves to the medical display, checks Lester's vitals, then enters a few commands.

"Two days," she says without looking back. "You'll be walking again in two days."

"But the deadline…" Lester starts to protest, still sounding like a drunk.

"Let me worry about that," she replies, then turns to Nick. Her stare cuts like glass. No words—just warning. "I have everything under control."

Nick swallows hard.

Tericia leans down and kisses Lester one more time, then heads out. Nick follows, but leaves distance between them.

She walks straight to the Holepunch, grabs a maintenance hammer, and circles around the rear panel.

Nick slows his pace, unsure.

Tericia glances back—then swings the hammer hard into the machinery.

CLANG.

"What the fuck are you doing?!" Nick shouts, rushing over. "Are you trying to get us killed?!"

He reaches for the hammer.

She spins, lifts the hammer, and levels it at him. "Try it and I will smash your skull in!" She shouts. "Now. Step. Back."

Nick freezes. Hands raised.

"Further," she commands, waving the hammer in his direction.

He steps back.

Tericia resumes—striking the same spot over and over until something inside snaps loose. A piece of the panel clatters to the floor.

She drops the hammer, bends, and picks it up.

"This needs to be replaced," she says, lifting the part into the light. "Only... the replacement doesn't exist yet."

Nick's eyes flicker from the broken part to her face. Something clicks in his mind. The tension in his body shifts—fear gives way to understanding.

And then... admiration.

"I see what you're doing," he says softly.

She tosses the part to him. He catches it.

"And," she says, voice lower now, "I have a plan to help you with your fucked up situation."

Nick stares at her—guilt, gratitude, and a strange hope forming all at once.

CHAPTER 10

Ten Years Ago...

"Welcome, everyone!"

The voice rings out with polished confidence, echoing in the pristine white space. Paul Burrdle stands at the front of the cleanroom, gleaming like a corporate poster child. His suit is tailored and blindingly blue, the purple shirt beneath it perfectly pressed. Black tie. Matching handkerchief. Hair clipped so precisely it might as well be stenciled on. Even his smile is weaponized—charming, symmetrical, and entirely intentional.

"It is an honor," Paul says, sweeping his arms wide, "to have you join the Borvil team."

Before him, twenty-three scientists and engineers stand shoulder to shoulder in identical white lab coats, buzzing with nervous excitement. The cleanroom around them shines under sterile lighting, with individual research pods lining the edges—glass-walled labs equipped with everything they could need. Each pod is its own pristine sanctuary of innovation.

The room hums with the quiet anticipation of possibility.

Behind Paul, a door slides open with a soft hiss.

"Before we proceed," he continues, "please welcome the mind behind the idea that sparked it all—Tericia Crut, project lead."

Tericia steps forward, hands folded tightly in front of her, her long brown hair tied back in a no-nonsense ponytail. She avoids eye contact. The room's attention feels like a weight pressing down on her shoulders.

Paul beams. "Tericia came to us with the concept for a stable wormhole generator. The kind that could revolutionize space travel. You've all been chosen— handpicked—for your talent, precision, and reputations. Together, you'll build the future."

There's a soft round of clapping. Some nods. Tericia gives a faint smile before backing away.

"Now," Paul says, clapping his hands, "please get to know each other, explore your pods, take inventory, and submit requests. Everything you need will be provided."

The group begins to disperse, voices rising in excitement as they approach the stations. Handshakes and smiles fill the room as they each introduce themselves as the walk.

Except for one.

"Randal Peterson." Paul's voice slices through the noise. "Please come with me. We've got a small issue to resolve."

Randal Peterson freezes for just a moment, surprised to hear his name. Then he smiles—still riding the high of being chosen for something revolutionary—and follows Paul out of the room. He waves goodbye to a few nearby colleagues, completely unaware that it may be the last time he ever sees them.

They walk down a bright corridor, turning left past a line of biometric scanners and sleek reinforced doors. Everything in this facility is polished, antiseptic, and cold.

Paul opens a door at the end of the hallway and gestures for Randal to enter.

The room is small and sterile, like a corporate interrogation chamber disguised as a high-end conference suite. No windows. Just two sleek chairs, a polished table, and a large screen on the wall behind Paul's seat.

"Have a seat," Paul says, the smile gone now—replaced by a detached professionalism that's far more chilling.

Randal obeys, nervousness blooming slowly in his chest.

Paul slides into the chair across from him, taps a command into the table interface, and the screen behind him flickers to life.

"We've noticed something concerning, Randal," Paul begins, folding his hands neatly. "Your NDA signature doesn't match the one on your other onboarding forms."

"Must have been excited about the project and just wanted to get all of the forms done. There were so many of them. I know this is secretive work and all, but that was excessive," Randal shares with a small laugh.

"We don't believe so. We need to know who you talked with. Who you shared the forms with. Who knows what you are doing here," Paul says bluntly.

"I…I don't know…what are you asking exactly?" Randal stammers, hoping to buy himself some time.

"If you are already in violation of this project, we need to know how badly you fucked up," Paul says without raising his voice.

"Why are you so serious about this? It's not like anyone will…"

"It's secretive for a reason," Paul interrupts. "We have done enough projects over the years to know what makes them a success and what leads to a disaster. We don't take chances. Now talk!"

Paul's sudden rise in temperament makes Randal choke down some spit.

Randal finally speaks, after looking around the room, Paul's eyes never looking away from Randal's. "I told my wife, her brother, and my parents. I was excited about the opportunity and wanted to share it with someone."

"Even after you were told not to?" Paul asks, making sure he understands Randal correctly. "Even after we were specific that not even your family should know."

"Yes. You said don't tell anyone, but I couldn't contain myself," Randal replies.

"And who saw the NDA? Why is the signature different?" Paul presses.

"Please. I don't know what you are talking about. That's my signature," Randal states, desperate for a resolution.

"So, what you are telling me is that either you signed the NDA and not the other documents, or you signed the other documents and not the NDA. Which one is it?" Paul asks, leaning forward, waiting for an answer. "Who has seen these documents?"

"I ca…" Randal pauses, unable to speak.

"You can't what?" Paul asks, pressing Randal into a confession.

"They'll kill my family," Randal states quickly.

"They can't," Paul replies confidently, sitting back into his chair, folding his hands again.

"You don't know the situation," Randal says nervously.

"That's why I am asking you," Paul replies.

"Look. I can't tell you or they die. Even if they were safe, I have to deliver. They signed it because I was hesitating when they..." Randal pauses.

"Held a gun to your wife's head?" Paul asks as though he already knows the story.

"What!? How?" Randal's confusion is nearly tangible, thick with questions.

"We. Don't. Take. Chances," Paul says each word slowly and clearly, then waves his hand across the table. The screen switches pictures and shows Randal's family bound and gagged in another room. "Like I said, they can't kill your family. But we can. And we can make you watch. Now give me what I want. I need names."

Randal's eyes go wide, he struggles to comprehend the situation.

"Randal. Name," Paul presses.

"But..." Randal wants to protest.

"Let me make this simple for you. Your family dies if I don't get a name. And if I still don't get a name, you die," Paul says bluntly, sitting back in his chair. "There is only one way out of this for you and your family. And, you have ten seconds to decide."

Randal looks at the screen and then back to Paul.

Paul starts counting the seconds.

Randal breaks within a few seconds. "Wait."

He stares into the screen one last time, then to the floor, then finally up at Paul.

"Praytose," he whispers.

"Yeah. Sounds like their standard operating procedure. Now, here is ours," Paul says, then stands, slowly, smoothly, and finally aims a gun at Randal and pulls the trigger. On the screen behind Paul, the security detail raises their guns and simultaneously pull their triggers. Randal and his family all dead in less than a second.

The room is silent, except for Paul's breathing. He calmly removes the black handkerchief from his pocket and wipes the weapon down, careful to polish it clean—making it look like new again.

He holsters the gun, straightens his tie.

"Not the start of the project I hoped for," he mutters.

A screen lights up on the far wall, and Tems's face appears, grainy and pale.

"I'm surprised there was only one breach," Tems says, voice cool and smooth. "Praytose will be disappointed. And I'm always pleased to contribute to said disappointment."

Paul nods. "What now?"

"Now?" Tems smirks. "Now we make them work fast. Use whatever tactics you like. I want this done as quickly as possible."

The screen goes black.

Paul glances once more at Randal's body, then turns to leave the room, his footfalls echoing in the cold, clinical silence.

CHAPTER 11

"Where is Randal?" Tericia asks as Paul returns to the main floor, his polished smile firmly back in place.

Paul blinks as though trying to recall a name from a list he doesn't care about. "Randal? Which one is he?"

"The one you pulled from the room during introductions," she says firmly, stepping into his path.

"Oh. Right. Randal," Paul says with a casual laugh. "Apologies, I've had a dozen people in my ear since then. So many names, it's hard to keep track."

"And?" she presses.

Paul clasps his hands behind his back. "He won't be joining the team after all."

"What?" Tericia's voice drops an octave, quiet and alarmed. "Will we get a replacement? He was potentially vital. His work on sub-entropic atomic structures—he knows more than anyone in the field."

Paul shrugs with a smile. "Not even sure what that means, but I'll see if I can scrounge up the second-best. For now? Count on no one else."

Before she can say another word, he pivots with mechanical precision. "Now if you'll excuse me, I must be on my way. And you've got a lot of work to do. We expect great things."

He walks away without a backward glance.

Tericia watches him go, her stomach tightening into a knot.

She mutters, "Already behind schedule, then."

The cleanroom bustles with subdued energy as the team begins to settle in. Scientists cluster into groups, claiming their pods, exploring the workbenches. Tericia moves through the room like a ghost in a dream she hasn't yet accepted is real—checking lists, approving supply requests, forcing herself to look composed.

"Lester Greenhard?" she calls as she approaches a larger pod off to the side.

He looks up from a table covered in dense equations. Lester's alone. His specialization—Quantum Topodynamics—is so niche that no other team was assigned to him. Tericia specifically requested him.

His dark eyes meet hers. Reserved. Gentle. Curious. Always a hint of fear behind them.

"Need anything?" she asks.

"You already thought of everything I could imagine. But I'll let you know if something comes up," he replies with a soft smile.

"I figured as much. I know our specialty too well not to over-prepare."

He nods again, his expression warm but cautious. She offers him a small, grateful smile before turning toward the front of the room.

She taps her tablet. The intercom chirps.

"Hello, everyone," she says into the mic. "A pleasure to meet you all. I've collected your requests and will pass them to management. Otherwise, call it a day. You're free to head out and get some rest. We'll begin fresh tomorrow."

She cuts the feed.

And then—

The intercom chirps again.

This time, a gruff male voice cuts through the air like a knife:

"Tericia Crut is not in charge—and never will be. Her dismissal of you for the day is misplaced. As noted in the documents you signed, you will not be leaving this facility until the project is complete. Dormitories are accessible through the south door. Anything you require from home will be retrieved for you. We don't want word of this place, and what you are doing, to get out. Secrecy must prevail."

The silence that follows is electric.

Tericia stares at the speaker, jaw slack. Her heart hammers in her chest.

Lester's eyes find hers from across the room.

Fear.

Dread.

Confusion.

"I'm sorry," she whispers, almost to herself. "I didn't know."

She rushes out of her pod and toward the main door. She attempts to open it but it doesn't budge.

She slams her fist on it. Nothing.

Frantically, she taps her tablet and hits the 'contact management' button.

A male voice answers, flat and unbothered. "What do you want?"

"This has to be a mistake," she says, trying to keep her voice even. "We were told this was a secure site, not a prison."

"You can either get to work or go to your dorm," the voice replies. "Those are your options."

"Why would anyone work under duress like this?" she demands.

"Because if you don't," the voice says coldly, "you won't get to do anything else."

The line goes dead.

Tericia stands there, stunned. "What does that mean?" She asks herself.

Slowly, she turns away from the door. The team has gathered behind her, having heard every word. Dozens of eyes stare at her, searching for answers. Demanding them.

"I'm sorry," she says, her voice shaking as she forces herself to project. "I was deceived. I didn't know this would happen. I never would've agreed to lead this project, and I certainly wouldn't have brought you here if I knew we'd be locked inside."

Murmurs rise into panicked whispers.

"We have families—"

"Is this legal—?"

"They can't just—"

Tericia raises her hands. "Please! I know you're scared. I am too. But panicking won't help. We'll work. We'll do the research. I'll fight for answers. I'll fight to get us out of here. I'll get us a different decision. Something."

Silence.

No one believes her—not yet.

But they want to.

She walks through the crowd without another word. They part for her like a slow-moving tide.

She heads through the south door, down a narrow hall to the dormitory wing. Glowing lights hum overhead. The air smells like sterilized sadness.

She finds her door.

Inside, there's a bed. A small sink mounted above a steel toilet. One overhead light. No windows. No décor.

Tericia sits on the edge of the bed, staring at the white wall across from her as she hears the voices of her colleagues filling the hall.

This isn't what she signed up for.

This isn't a lab.

It's a cage.

CHAPTER 12

Ten Years Ago + 30 Days

"We aren't getting anywhere under these conditions. And without Randal—"

"Tericia, shut up."

Mark Mult's interruption slices through the air like a blade. He doesn't raise his voice—he never has to. His cold, precise tone is more threatening than yelling could ever be.

"Your excuses are the problem," he continues, pacing behind her like a warden evaluating livestock. "Not the conditions. Not the loss of one incompetent scientist. The problem... is you."

Tericia stands rigid, arms crossed, jaw clenched. Mark is Borvil's true enforcer—Paul Burrdle was the velvet glove; Mark is the iron fist. He watches everything. Questions everything. Doubts everyone.

"We expected results," he says. "You sold this project as viable. Thirty days in, and what do we have? Nothing. So, let's try a new approach. Tell me which team member is dragging the rest down."

The words land like a toxin in the room.

Tericia's breath catches. She looks up at him, disbelieving. "Excuse me?"

"I said," he repeats, voice like static, "name someone. Or we'll pick at random."

She stares at him.

"You are the problem. Paul is the problem. This Tems guy is the problem," she finally says, crossing her arms.

"You're funny and wrong. Name a name or we will pick someone at random," Mark says.

Paul was ruthless, but Mark? Mark is surgical.

"I—I can't just—" She glances around the cleanroom complex. Through the glass, scientists hunch over instruments, deep in their work, or pretending to be. Every window feels like a mirror. Every colleague a potential sacrifice.

Mark raises an eyebrow. "Tick tock."

Her heart slams against her ribs. She doesn't want to say it. But silence, here, is worse than betrayal.

"...Trenton Gill," she finally whispers. "He means well, but... he's in the way more than he helps."

Mark nods without a word, taps something into his tablet.

A moment later, the door to the cleanroom hisses open.

Two guards in black armor enter.

"No," Tericia says softly, and ultimately too late.

They march straight to Trenton's pod.

People start to rise from their seats, uncertain. Then they see the guns.

"Wait, what is—?!" Trenton starts to say, startled as the guards seize his arms. They drag him out of the pod and into Tericia's pod, near Mark and Tericia.

Mark doesn't move. Doesn't look at Trenton. His eyes remain locked on Tericia. But he does raise his hand, letting the guards know that they have moved Trenton far enough.

The guards turn Trenton around to face the team. Each one of them staring at what is happening. Each one's gaze looking right at Trenton, the guards, Tericia, and Mark.

One of the guards raises a pistol. Tenton's eyes pleading for help.

"No—!" someone shouts.

The shot is deafening.

Trenton's head snaps to the side as the bullet tears through it. Blood sprays in a perfect arc across the white pod wall. His body crumples. Red pools where sterile flooring gleamed.

Silence.

Mark smiles faintly having never taken his eyes off of Tericia's.

"Get this project done," he says, stepping over Trenton's body as though it's nothing. "Or your team will keep getting smaller."

The door hisses closed behind him as he and the guards leave.

Within seconds, the pod floods with voices. The team rushes in from all directions, questions and accusations spilling over each other like a rising tide.

"Tericia—what just happened?"

"Why him?"

"Did you know they'd do that?"

"What the hell is going on?"

But Tericia doesn't answer.

She doesn't even hear them—not fully. Their words are distant echoes, muffled by the pounding of her own heartbeat in her ears. She rises slowly from her seat, limbs heavy with disbelief, and begins to move.

The crowd parts instinctively as she walks through them. The noise falls away behind her, fading into a dull hum. Every step toward Trenton's body drags like walking through molasses. Her breath catches. Her legs tremble.

She said his name.

She gave them a target.

She pulled the trigger, even if she never touched the gun.

She could have resisted. Could have named no one. Could've offered herself. The guilt coils around her ribs like a vice.

She reaches Trenton's lifeless form.

Blood paints the sterile white floor in harsh, jarring reds. It's already pooling near his outstretched fingers. Tericia drops to her knees beside him, her breath stolen, her senses numb.

She wants to scream—but her voice won't come.

She wants to cry—but no tears fall.

She wants to run—but her body is stone.

She just stares.

It isn't until a warm hand lands gently on her shoulder that she blinks. The numbness flickers. She lifts her head.

Lester.

His eyes are soft, his voice a hush that barely reaches her through the fog.

"This sucks," he says quietly. "That's all there is to it. And nothing anyone says will change how you feel right now. But just know—nobody here blames you. You didn't know. None of us did."

Her lower lip quivers. Finally, the tears come, trembling free as her eyes meet his. She turns, taking in the crowd now gathered in stunned silence. All those expectant faces. Grieving. Afraid. Waiting for her.

She forces herself to stand.

Her voice barely breaks the quiet: "I'm sorry."

And then she lowers her head and weeps.

Lester steps beside her, offering silent support. After a moment, he asks gently, "Did he tell you how to stop this from happening again?"

Tericia nods faintly, her voice barely audible. "Finish the project."

A tense murmur spreads through the group.

"Do they even know how long real science takes?" someone says, voice rising with disbelief.

"Fabricating parts can take weeks—months."

"And that's just to test one subsystem," another adds. "It's not just one invention. It's thousands of micro-inventions that all have to work together."

"It could take years!" a voice shouts from the back. "We won't survive that long!"

The unease thickens into panic. Despair hangs heavy in the air.

Tericia doesn't try to answer. She doesn't have the strength—or the truth that would comfort them. She turns and walks slowly toward the dormitory corridor. The crowd doesn't follow. They just watch her go, haunted and hollow.

She reaches the door, passes through it, and disappears into the long, quiet hallway, needing what none of them can offer: answers… and peace.

And she has neither.

Later, Tericia sits alone with Mark in her pod.

He drinks something from a sleek metal thermos, staring out at nothing.

"I just want to say thank you," she begins, carefully.

Mark glances sideways.

"I should've made clearer from the beginning how long this project will take," she continues. "Science isn't a switch. It's a process. If you keep scaring people, they'll make mistakes. The project will fall apart."

Mark nods slightly.

"I'll make sure everyone stays motivated," she adds. "But I need your word that no one else dies. We're trying to build the future, not burn it down."

He stands slowly, leans close, and whispers something only she hears:

"My concessions have cost me everything."

Before she can respond, he turns and walks away.

She watches him exit the pod. At the end of the hallway, a man waits.

Tall. Stern.

Tems.

Mark slows, exchanges no words. Tems motions with a jerk of his chin.

The door hisses closed behind them.

Tericia never sees Mark again.

CHAPTER 13

Nine Years Ago

"We're done with delays," Tems growls, voice pressed close to Tericia's ear. He stands behind her like a shadow come alive, bent forward so his breath grazes her skin. "Turn the fucking thing on."

Tericia's hands hover above a console, frozen. Her shoulders lock, spine straight. His presence hums like a high-voltage wire.

"We're making progress," she says carefully. "Real progress. Parts are coming together. But this isn't a light switch—it's a wormhole. Gravity, atomic expansion, atomic destabilization, fourth-dimensional collapse, other unknowns we can't even begin to understand—we're threading a cosmic needle with a blindfold on."

Tems says nothing. The silence is worse than any reply.

"You want us to turn on something that could swallow the planet? Trigger quantum feedback, a chain reaction, collapse a system of worlds we've never seen? You want that?"

She turns slightly, meeting his gaze.

"I don't see how that's profitable."

He doesn't answer.

He just straightens his suit with mechanical grace, turns, and walks out of the pod.

Then—

Bang.

A single shot cracks down the sterile white hall. Tericia flinches and runs toward the sound.

Rachel Ulter lies crumpled on the floor. Her face is gone. A bloom of red splashes across the floor like spilled ink. Tems walks past the body without slowing down, tucking the gun away like it's nothing more than a pen.

"Tems!" Tericia screams. "How the fuck are we supposed to make progress when you keep doing this?!"

The door hisses shut behind him.

That night, the lounge is thick with fear and grief. The dormitory lights are dimmed, casting long shadows across pale faces.

"What do we do now?" Edward Polling asks, his voice shaking.

"Yeah! We're making progress. What the hell does he want?" Sara Hoytle murmurs.

Tericia steps forward before the spiral begins. "He wants us to turn the device on."

A murmur ripples through the group.

"It's not ready," Ventro Palice says. He sounds more exhausted than angry. "It won't do anything yet. It took twenty years to build the Large Hadron Collider, granted half of that was just digging the tunnel. Still."

"We all know that," Tericia replies. "I told him—again—that jumping the gun could result in a planetary catastrophe. But he either doesn't care or doesn't believe me. Maybe both."

She pauses. Then, despite herself, a faint smile flickers on her face. "Which, I guess, is ironic… given gravity is half our problem."

It's not a joke, not really. But it cuts the tension for a second. A breath, then a crash.

"He's killed two others this year," Garrison Mathers says quietly.

Tericia nods. "And I've told him every time—it sets us back. Fear isn't motivating anyone. When we thought the executions were over? That brief calm? We made real progress. We remembered how to have hope."

Tericia pauses before continuing, "I remember the first day we were here, before they took anyone away. I was so nervous. But excited. Ready to innovate. Ready to take on the biggest and best project humanity has ever seen. I was eager to make real lasting change for humanity. To build peace and prosperity for everyone in the universe."

"But that's not the world he wants," Lester adds from across the room. "He doesn't care about science. He doesn't care about peace and prosperity for all. He just wants power."

Everyone's gaze shifts to Lester.

"Let's leave Tericia alone," Lester adds gently. "She's carrying the weight of all of us. She is taking the brunt of this from Tems."

"Thanks, Lester," Tericia says, meeting his gaze. "But I'm the lead. This burden is mine. Let them vent. If it buys them one more night of sleep, it's worth it."

Silence falls again, thicker than before.

She stands. "Get some rest. Tomorrow doesn't wait."

The next day, in the hum of the lab pod, Lester and Tericia work in near silence. Data floats across the displays like silent snowfall.

"Do you think we'll ever finish this?" Lester asks, eyes flicking toward her.

"I don't think about that," she replies without looking up. "I just move forward."

Lester's hands pause above a control interface. "Every time someone dies, it gets a little closer to being one of us."

"I know," she says. "And I hate that we've all learned to accept it."

A knock at the door. Tericia's heart jumps in fear, every pore on her body opens, and she looks up.

Maggie Sprink stands there—stoic, still. Her eyes are sunken, movements mechanical. The brilliant robotics specialist now walks like a ghost of her former self.

"Yes, Maggie?" Tericia asks softly, doing her best to keep the adrenaline at bay.

"We've completed the initial assembly. Ready for the first test."

Her voice is barely a whisper.

"Thank you. I'll be right there."

Tericia rises. "Maybe we're closer than we thought," she mutters to herself.

The test room smells like dust and sterilized metal. A half dozen team members surround the device. Screens flicker. Gears hum.

Tericia steps to the console and looks at the displays. She eyes each readout making sure nothing causes her to second guess this small, yet significant test.

Maggie checks the last connections. The team waits, some clearly holding their breath.

Tericia nods to Maggie who taps the command.

The machine awakens, humming like a living thing. The first laser fires, invisible to the eye. A hiss of steam rises from the invisible line in the air, a trail of smoke the only visible indication that it is on. The laser set to its lowest possible setting.

She adds a tenth of a microgram of biryliandioxide to the chamber—barely a shimmer, smaller than a flake of dust.

Sensors flare to life. Readouts begin scrolling. The wall of displays above them glows with incoming data. The target at the end of the pod surrounding by a vast array of sensors measuring every energy spectrum, magnetism, gravitational anomalies, and more. Graphs, waveforms, radiation spikes all report their findings.

It worked. Something happened. The test only lasts for a few seconds before Tericia turns off the device.

Before anyone can speak—

A voice cuts through the air like a blade.

"What's the verdict?"

Everyone jolts.

Tems is in the room.

Tericia turns slowly to face him. Everyone else averts their eyes.

"We just ran the test," she says. "It will take time to interpret the data. Could be a week. Maybe more."

"I'm growing impatient."

She furrows her brow. "You mean you weren't impatient before?"

Tems takes a step forward.

"Are you testing me, Tericia?"

Her jaw tightens.

"Tems," she says, steady but exhausted, "I've told you a hundred ways. You can't rush this. And you can't beat science into submission. The only thing you've killed by killing people—is progress."

She pauses.

"But you don't care about that, do you?"

"Finish your thought," Tems says, voice like poisoned silk as he takes another step toward Tericia.

"It doesn't matter," she replies, looking down. "You don't listen."

Tems steps even closer, just a breath away now. "Oh, but I do."

He gestures toward the door.

Eight new scientists enter, all smiles, all hope.

Fresh blood.

Disposable minds.

"You brought new people," Tericia says, stunned.

Tems leans in. "Call it a backup plan. Or target practice. Your progress will decide their fate."

Tericia turns away, shaking with fury. "You're a fucking monster."

She storms toward the exit. He follows. The moment she turns the corner, he grabs her by the wrist, spins her into the wall, slamming her head and back hard against its surface.

His hand closes around her throat.

"You want to see a monster?" he hisses, lips brushing her ear. "Keep testing me."

Her vision blurs.

He stares at her with hollow eyes.

Empty.

Hungry.

And then, he lets go.

She drops to her knees, gasping.

He turns back toward the others and says in a raised voice, "Make sure you bring your new colleagues up to speed on how I run things around here. Maybe that will keep the monster at bay."

He looks back down at her, half-smiling, then walks away.

The main door hisses closed as Tems walks out.

The newcomers stand frozen in the hallway, their earlier excitement now curdled into pure confusion and dread.

Tericia coughs, pulls herself upright against the wall, and wipes a trembling hand across her mouth.

The newcomers stand near Tericia, befuddled looks on their faces.

"Welcome to hell," she mutters to herself, only she realizes she said it loudly enough for the new people to hear.

CHAPTER 14

Eight Years Ago...

The lab feels emptier than ever.

The science station that once pulsed with energy—alive with discussion, clatter, and innovation—along with fear, doubt, and frustration—is now a tomb of echoes and faded dreams. The team is down to four. Every failure meant someone's death. Every delay, another punishment. Every request was met with violence. Being held captive wasn't enough for Tems. He needed more—needed to break them.

And he did.

Tericia, Lester, Charles, and Willa now sit hunched on sagging couches in the main living area, the sterile white walls pressing in like a padded cell. They've just come from another brutal day. Another round of threats. Another ultimatum.

"I might just beat them to the punch," Charles mutters, voice like ash.

"Don't say that," Lester replies, though his voice lacks conviction. "We might still get out. We might still finish this."

The hope rings false.

"Doubtful," Willa says quietly, her eyes hollow.

Tericia leans forward, arms resting on her knees. "I wish I'd never brought my research to Borvil. I should've seen the signs. The NDA. The isolation. The silence."

"Don't you dare," Lester says, cutting her off. "What you discovered—what we're building—matters. It could change everything. The cost shouldn't have been this high, but now that we're here… we survive. We finish. No matter what. The four of us, we can survive. We just make sure we are all so vital to the solution that he can't afford to kill anymore."

His words hang in the air like ghosts.

No one speaks.

No one has to.

They all want to see a wormhole. They all want to pass through it. But deep down, none of them believe they'll live long enough.

One by one, they rise and drift off toward their assigned bunks. Silent goodnights. Exhausted glances.

The night swallows the rest.

The months that follow blur together.

Progress is made, but never fast enough for Tems. The machine hums to life, but the results don't match his expectations.

Charles and Willa pay the price.

They are executed without ceremony. Without reason. Just like the countless lives before.

Now it's just Tericia and Lester.

"I'm running out of targets," Tems sneers as he polishes his weapon, Willa's blood still drying on the wall behind him. She had smiled at him just before the shot—a final act of defiance that only seemed to amuse him more.

"Shall I bring me some more?" he asks, eyes glinting like shattered obsidian.

Tericia doesn't even flinch anymore. Her voice is cold steel. "Do what you want. Just… leave Lester and me alone. We're making progress. We can finish it."

Tems tilts his head. "When?"

"We don't know how long it will take," Lester says, stepping in before Tericia can answer.

It's a mistake.

Tericia sees Tems shift, eyes narrowing. She doesn't even have time to warn him.

Tems moves like a serpent—silent and fast. He steps in and drives his heel into Lester's leg. A sickening snap echoes through the lab.

Lester screams, crumpling to the floor, clutching his leg as agony overtakes him.

Tems crouches beside him, voice venomous. "Don't. Ever. Interrupt me again."

He stands, brushes off his suit, and glances back at Tericia with a smirk. "Don't make me regret sparing him."

And then he's gone.

The next few years stretch into a purgatory of survival and work. Tericia and Lester are left to rebuild the project—just the two of them. No replacements. No team.

Progress slows. They have to learn everything themselves. Every wire, every equation, every discipline once handled by other scientists is now split between two exhausted people held together by habit, trauma, and unspoken loyalty. Loyalty to each other. Loyalty to the science.

Sometimes Tems shows up.

They never know when.

Sometimes he brings a stranger—a homeless man, a prisoner, an unlucky soul—and throws the body into the room. Then he opens fire, emptying a magazine while staring directly at Tericia, daring her to react. Reminding them of the power he wields.

Sometimes it's just one shot to the head.

Sometimes it's the whole clip.

Always silence after.

The lab has an incinerator, originally designed to destroy failed prototypes, sensitive data, broken components, and lethal compounds. A way to dispose of company secrets so they don't fall into the wrong hands. Unfortunately, it has become something else entirely.

Tericia took it upon herself to be the one who moved the bodies to the incinerator. Lester finally started helping after his leg healed.

"I don't even know who this person is," Tericia mutters, her voice dulled by repetition as they roll another body toward the incinerator. "What's the point of this?"

Lester doesn't speak. He just mouths a single word.

'Sociopath.'

They say nothing more. They know the lab is wired, their conversations monitored.

Tericia blinks slowly—acknowledging, agreeing, saying everything she needs to with that one gesture.

They push the cart to the edge of the incinerator door and slide the body in.

The door shuts with a mechanical certainty.

The flames roar to life.

The silence returns.

Then they go back to their pod.

Back to the work.

Back to pretending that this—all of this—is still for something greater.

Until one day, at last, the machine, the wormhole device, lovingly called Holepunch, is complete.

And they go into the void.

CHAPTER 15

"How long have you known?" Lester asks, his voice soft, almost cautious.

Tericia doesn't look at him. Her eyes stay fixed on the display in front of her.

"Took me about a day to figure it out," she replies after a few moments.

"No. I mean—when exactly? What triggered it?" Lester presses.

Tericia exhales slowly. "Nick's idea. Adjusting the wormhole's focal points to change size. That was the breakthrough. From there… it was just a matter of connecting dots. A day later, I knew."

Lester shifts in his chair, processing the weight of that. "And you didn't say anything. You just, what?… let Tems believe we were still stumbling in the dark?"

"Yeah. You could have prevented Lester's leg from being shot," Nick snaps, stepping into the conversation with rising frustration. "You could've solved all of this. Solved all of our problems. But you didn't. You knew how to make the wormhole go anywhere in the galaxy, and you did nothing."

"Solve our problems?" Tericia's voice turns sharp, cutting. "Are you fucking serious?"

Nick blinks.

"Your orders were to kill us once the solution was found," she continues, stepping forward, jaw clenched. "And you think solving this is the end of our problems? No, Nick. That's when they start. You've seen what Borvil is. What Tems is. The second this becomes viable tech, it becomes a weapon. They'll commercialize it, militarize it, patent the stars. Space travel, colonization, control—everything will be theirs. Entire civilizations reduced to footnotes in profit margins. They will dictate their own laws. They will do whatever they want because they can appear and disappear across the galaxy like someone walking through a door. Only that door can be anywhere and appear anywhere. Nobody will be safe. Nobody will have a choice."

She pauses, breathing heavy. "And Tems... Tems will be the fucking emperor of it all."

Silence hangs like a knife.

"...Hey," Lester says abruptly, changing the subject, "did we ever bring Parmen back?"

"Nope," Tericia replies, casually now. "I sabotaged the duplicate device before we had a chance. Been slowly patching it together ever since."

"Well," Lester says, shifting again, "maybe we could do that instead. You know... less getting shot, more retrieval of Parmens."

"Can't," Tericia says flatly.

Both men turn to her.

"The moment we activate it, Tems will be watching. Tracking everything. We open a wormhole, he opens a command channel. No. I have a better plan."

She turns her back to them and begins tapping on the console, her fingers moving with purpose. From a narrow crevice beneath the workstation, she pulls out a small metallic device—sleek, compact, and unmarked.

Lester and Nick exchange a look, mirrored shrugs passing silently between them.

Tericia's smile is faint but real. "We're done playing his game."

She presses a final command.

A wormhole tears open three meters in front of them. But it doesn't reveal space—no stars, no blackness. Instead, on the other side of the shimmering threshold, sits a man in a chair. Alone. Lit by sterile lighting. Surrounded by silence.

Tems.

He lifts his head, startled. "What the—?"

Tericia steps forward and hurls the device through the wormhole.

It lands at his feet.

His eyes flash wide.

"What is the meaning of this!?" he bellows, rising halfway from his chair.

Tericia doesn't answer. She lifts a small remote in her hand and presses the trigger.

The wormhole collapses.

Gone.

"What… was that?" Lester asks, still blinking in disbelief.

"Let's just say," Tericia answers, returning to the console, "Nick's problem is about to be solved. And our primary tormentor is about to experience the very technology he abused."

Nick's breath catches. "Wait… what did you do?"

"Repositioned his atoms," Tericia says coolly. "Tems should now be spread about as thin as paint on the wall."

Tericia and Nick stare, unsure they heard her correctly.

"Bomb. Explosion. His body no longer being intact. Blood painting the walls. Any of this make sense now?" Tericia asks, cutting through any confusion.

They nod and small smiles start to form on their faces.

Tericia then turns toward Nick, calm and resolute. "Where's your family?"

Nick hesitates. "They're at our home. Under guard. Two men outside the house. Always."

"Pull up the location," Tericia says, pointing to the navigation display on the device.

Nick does, hands shaking slightly. He brings it up on the map. Tericia scans it, nods once, then adjusts Holepunch again. New coordinates. New interface settings. She executes the command.

A second wormhole appears—this time revealing the inside of a modest home. A couch. A flickering TV. And Nick's wife and daughters, frozen in confusion, looking straight into the mouth of the unknown.

"Go," Tericia commands.

Nick bolts through the wormhole without hesitation. He puts a finger to his lips, urging his family to stay quiet, then kneels and embraces them with shaking arms. He whispers something, urgent but soft. They listen. They trust.

Hand in hand, they step through.

Tericia closes the wormhole just as a guard bursts into the room behind them, running at top speed to chase Nick through.

Half of one guard makes it.

The front half—arm, shoulder, torso, leg—falls to the floor in a grisly thud, blood spraying across the sterile floor.

The daughters scream. Nick pulls them close, shielding their eyes.

Lester stumbles back, gagging, nearly losing it but managing to stay upright.

Tericia… doesn't flinch.

She stares at the remains, calm. Composed. Cold.

A decision hardens in her eyes. One that's been forming for years.

No more.

No more deaths. No more obedience. No more giving humanity's greatest discovery to the monsters who would twist it into a throne of bones.

Her fingers tighten into a fist. Her breath steadies.

A small, dangerous smile curves her lips.

Change is coming. Borvil won't get what they want. They will get karma instead.

And this time, science will write the rules.

CHAPTER 16

The wormhole opens with a soft vibration, light refracting around the edges like ripples of liquid glass. Tericia leans toward the console, eyes locked on the swirling portal.

"Parmen," she says clearly, her voice steady but urgent. "Sorry for the delay. Please return before the wormhole closes."

Lester crosses his arms as he stands behind her, watching the display. "He could be dead at this point," he mutters, more to himself than anyone else.

Tericia doesn't flinch. "Maybe. But he had enough rations, water, and oxygen to last this long. He's smart. He knows how to wait."

Nick steps forward, brow furrowed. "He might've wandered. Drifted off. Started exploring. He could be kilometers away by now."

Tericia whirls around, cutting him off with a sharp glare. "Stop telling me what I already know," she snaps. "We don't have time for hypotheticals. He could be minutes away or on the other side of the system. You two need to worry more about Borvil coming up here. Monitor the displays to see if they are. And until we can get weapons to defend ourselves…" she glances back at the display, fingers hovering over the controls. Her tone shifts slightly, less harsh now, more calculating, "we will…have…to…"

"Parmen, I have to shut the wormhole. If you see this message—head to the probe I'm leaving. We'll open another wormhole in less than an hour. Just stay near it. Don't move."

She deploys a probe, watching as it drifts into the portal and disappears. Then, without hesitation, she closes the wormhole with a single tap.

Lester exhales through his nose. "So, what now?"

Tericia doesn't answer immediately. She's already bringing up her mapping system, her fingers dancing across the interface with precision. Coordinates populate the screen, crosshairs zooming in toward a facility nestled within a forested military zone.

She stares at it for a beat. Then she speaks—calmly, almost too calmly. "Now, we stop waiting around and arm ourselves."

Nick blinks. "Wait… is that—?"

"A weapons storage facility," Lester finishes, realization dawning. His eyes widen slightly. "Tericia… are you serious?"

Tericia nods once, then executes the command.

The wormhole opens again, this time revealing a dim, utilitarian hallway lined with locked crates and supply racks. The air on the other side pulses with sterile, manufactured cold. glowing lights flicker overhead.

"Move," she commands. "Take what you can carry. If it's too much, drag it on a cart. We are not fighting empty-handed."

Without waiting for them to react, Tericia strides forward, steps through the wormhole, and emerges inside the facility. She grabs the first laser rifle she sees, checks the charge, and flicks the safety off. Then, without a word, she steps back through.

"Now go," she says, tossing the rifle onto the floor beside her. "I'll manage the portal. If anything goes wrong, I'll close it."

Lester and Nick exchange a look. Then Lester jerks his head forward. "Let's go."

They cross the wormhole threshold. Moments later, crates and weapons begin to pile on the lab floor in rapid succession—plasma rifles, pulse grenades, portable ion mines, and stacks of ammunition.

Tericia hustles to move the stockpile out of the line of fire, dragging gear with a strength born of adrenaline and purpose. Her lab coat flaps with every sharp motion, her breathing controlled but intense.

"Grab more explosives!" she shouts through the portal. "We want them to know we're not fucking around. And I don't have time to create my own."

Lester rummages through a nearby rack, his hands finding a case marked with a hazard warning. "High-yield, low-weight. Perfect," he mutters, then shoves it through the wormhole. Nick follows close behind, arms full of incendiary grenades and energy-cell packs.

Five minutes pass. The pile of weapons grows, neatly stacked by Tericia into makeshift barricades. The air is thick with tension.

Then it hits.

BLAAA... BLAAA... BLAAA...

The security alarm blares from within the facility—an earsplitting klaxon that echoes across the steel walls and right through the wormhole.

"Shit!" Lester yells from inside. "Is that because of us!?"

"Let's not take chances! Get back here!" Tericia screams.

Nick leaps through first, a duffle bag slung over his shoulder. He tumbles onto the lab floor and drops the bag, eyes wide with panic.

Tericia draws her rifle and takes cover behind a stacked crate of energy cells, finger poised on the trigger.

Lester is still inside, dragging a final case toward the wormhole when the door on the far end of the depot slams open.

A dozen soldiers flood into the room, weapons raised.

"DROP IT! ON THE GROUND, NOW!" one of them shouts, the others spreading in a practiced arc.

Lester freezes mid-step. His eyes lock with Tericia's. There's no time. No words.

"Hold your fire," a commanding voice yells. "What the fuck is that thing?"

A soldier spots the wormhole and hesitates. He raises his weapon toward it, eyes narrowing—he sees the swirling light and a woman on the other side.

Tericia pulls the trigger.

The soldier's face bursts into red mist.

Gasps echo in the depot. Chaos erupts.

"SHOTS FIRED!"

Two more soldiers spin toward the wormhole.

Tericia ducks, squeezing off two more rounds. Missed. Shouts fill the air.

Nick drops to the floor, crawling toward the edge of the console.

"STOP SHOOTING, GODDAMN IT!" the commanding officer roars. "Explosives!"

"Let him go!" Tericia shouts. "Let Lester through and we walk away."

"Not a chance," the officer snarls. "We don't negotiate with terrorists!"

Nick takes aim. A soldier near Lester—the one watching him too closely—stands in his sights.

He hesitates. His finger trembles.

Tericia turns and meets his gaze. Her eyes tell him everything: Do it.

Nick swallows hard, nods once, and fires.

Another burst of crimson. Another body hits the floor.

Gunfire rains back toward the wormhole. Tericia drops behind the crates.

A soldier rushes forward and opens fire, ignoring his commander's orders.

"STOP SHOOTING OR I'LL PUT YOU DOWN MYSELF!" the officer bellows.

Tericia crawls to the console and begins typing furiously.

"Let. Him. Go," she snarls.

"No deal!" the officer replies.

She hits execute.

The wormhole closes.

Lester freezes, surrounded. He hears the silence now—the absence of escape. He's alone, hands raised, body trembling. Soldiers close in. His thoughts start to betray him. 'Did she just leave me to die? To take the wrap for this? Is this how it ends for me?'

Then—another wormhole flashes open behind him.

Tericia and Nick stand on the other side.

Two quick shots ring out. Chaos resumes, the soldiers scatter, looking for cover.

Lester doesn't think—he dives backward. Nick grabs his shoulder and yanks him through. They crash to the ground in the lab, breathless.

Tericia scrambles to the console as shots fly toward them. One zings past her shoulder. She drops, rolls, and slams her palm onto the panel.

The wormhole vanishes with a hiss.

Silence.

Breathless, the three of them lie sprawled on the floor.

"Are you okay?" Nick pants, crawling toward Tericia.

She holds up her lab coat. A smoking hole cuts through the fabric—but not her skin.

"I'll need a new coat," she says with a smirk, breath ragged. "But I'm alive."

Lester crawls to her and wraps his arms around her, trembling. "You saved me."

"I wasn't going to leave you behind," she whispers.

They hold each other for a long moment. Then Tericia stands and returns to the console.

She enters new coordinates.

A new wormhole opens, revealing deep space.

Parmen's ship waits beside the beacon probe—exactly where they left it.

Nick and Lester stare, wide-eyed.

Tericia turns to them, her eyes shining with steel-hard resolve.

"Now," she says, "we make a statement."

CHAPTER 17

"Say that again?" Parmen leans forward, his face twisted in confusion.

"Dead," Tericia says, her voice firm. "He's dead. Tems is dead. Do you understand that part?"

Parmen blinks, stunned. "Yes... I heard you. But—how?"

Tericia doesn't blink. She doesn't look away. "He left you to die, Parmen. Do you understand that part?"

Parmen scoffs, frustrated. "Yes, I fucking get that! He abandoned me. I knew that the moment the wormhole closed. But I want to know how he died."

"He used you like a tool," she continues, ignoring his question entirely. Her tone sharpens, more forceful. "He sent you out there with no guarantee of return. You were expendable. You still are to Borvil. That's who they are."

"Yes, I know all that!" Parmen growls. "But how did Tems die? What happened?!"

Tericia doesn't answer. She leans forward slightly, keeping her focus laser-sharp. "Borvil doesn't care about you. They never did. That's the part that matters. You were a statistic to them—a bullet point in a mission report."

Parmen throws his arms up, exasperated. "Fine! I give up. I get it. I'm not an idiot."

Lester interjects, his tone calmer. "Where did the wormhole open when you tried to return? Did you reach Earth?"

Parmen's jaw tightens. "I don't know. All I can tell you is that it wasn't back here. It wasn't Earth. The stars looked and felt unfamiliar. I've seen every chart in the Terran Fleet archives, and I didn't recognize that quadrant. But there was a planet."

The room changes instantly.

"A planet?!" Tericia, Lester, and Nick all exclaim at once, leaning forward.

"Inhabited?" Nick blurts out.

"Gas giant?" Lester asks quickly.

"How big was it?" Tericia demands.

Parmen holds up his hands like a traffic cop. "Whoa, whoa—calm the fuck down. One question at a time. And since you haven't even answered my question, why should I answer any of yours?"

Nick stands, crossing his arms. "She killed Tems. She had to. It was the only way to save my family. Now answer our questions about the planet!"

Parmen's eyes narrow. "You?" He turns to Tericia, pointing. "You—capable of murder? That's hard to imagine."

"It's true," Lester says, without a hint of hesitation. "Now answer our questions."

"You two would be terrible captives," Tericia mutters, shaking her head. "Haven't even been tortured and you're already giving away the whole story."

"We have been tortured," Lester counters, grinning faintly. "But we found a planet, Tericia. A new world! That changes everything."

"I agree," Nick says, eyes bright. "But Parmen still hasn't told us what we need to know."

Parmen sighs. "Looked habitable. That's all I got. I didn't go through. No probes, no scans. I wasn't going to risk getting stuck in some part of space with no way to return or even be found."

Lester can't sit still anymore. "Tericia… whatever your plan is, it can wait. We need to see that planet."

Tericia nods, her voice resolute. "Agreed. We've got both devices. We know how to target a location. We're going to that planet."

Parmen steps in front of the exit, arms crossed. "I'm not with you. You've admitted to murder and now to stealing privately funded property. And that pile of weapons near you doesn't look legit either. I'm not interested in going rogue. I'm not going to prison for you. I'm not going to die for some side quest. I get paid well by Borvil to risk my life."

Tericia's gaze hardens. "You're seriously still loyal to them? After they used you like throwaway cutlery?"

Parmen doesn't flinch. "I knew what I was signing up for. I accepted the risks. What I want is to go down in history. First human through a wormhole. That matters to me."

Tericia steps closer, lowering her voice. "You're a soldier. You believe in honor, in doing what's right. Tell me, is blindly serving a corrupt corporate regime part of that?"

"They won't kill me," Parmen says, almost as if trying to convince himself. "Why would they?"

"Because you've seen too much," Tericia answers immediately. "Because you could talk. Even accidentally. Say the wrong thing in an interview, mention the wrong detail, and they'll erase you. If you aren't already gone before getting the chance. Remember, They. Don't. Take. Chances."

He frowns but doesn't respond.

"They need this tech to be perfect," Tericia continues, her tone sharpening like a blade. "To be safe. To be clean. A hero stranded in space? That's a PR disaster."

Parmen swallows, his expression darkening.

"Tell me I'm wrong," she challenges. "Tell me you wouldn't laugh about it in a bar, let the story slip. Then you'd be explaining how you got rescued. Then you'd be talking about us. Everything would unravel for them."

"Okay. Fine. You're right," he says at last, voice quiet.

Tericia straightens. "So, you're either with us—or you're a liability." Tericia pauses a long time before and after accusing Parmen of being a liability. She wants him to really think about what a liability might mean in this situation.

Parmen nods slowly. "I get it. I do. I'm just… disappointed. I wanted this to mean something."

"It still can," Tericia says, her voice steady. "But only if you live to tell the story. You're already the first human to travel through a wormhole—that legacy is yours. But help us now, and you won't just be remembered… you'll be legendary. The first to discover a new world."

"That'll definitely write you into history," Lester adds. "Right next to Galileo, Einstein, Armstrong."

"I see what you're trying to do. You want me to side with you and use my training as a soldier to help you fight Borvil," Parmen replies.

Tericia simply smiles in return and whispers, "legendary" while arching her hands over her head in slow motion.

Parmen's expression cracks into a smile.

Nick joins in, voice soft but sincere. "And you'll get to tell your own story. Without censorship. Without consequences. You'll control the narrative."

Parmen exhales and lifts his head. "All right. I'm in. Let's go see that planet. Fuck Borvil."

With two ships prepped and fully armed, and each fitted with its own wormhole generator, the crew departs.

Parmen rides with Tericia in one vessel. Lester, Nick, and Nick's family ride in the other, sitting side-by-side in the command seats, watching the swirling glow of the freshly-opened wormhole.

Parmen's ship leads the way—its wormhole generator still in its original state, no modifications, no targeting calibration. Just as it was when he first used it.

The wormhole pulses open before them. The black void stretches beyond, ringed with vibrating violet light.

"This still feels insane," Lester mutters as he watches the borders shimmer.

"You did refill the Xomithrine cells, right?" he asks Nick.

Nick nods. "Filled both tanks before we launched. We've got enough for a round trip and then some."

"Good," Lester says, finally relaxing into the seat. "Because if we get stranded five thousand light-years from Earth over a math error, I'm going to haunt you forever."

The wormhole snaps shut behind them.

Silence.

Open space surrounds them—silent, cold, and distant. Stars stare back in unfamiliar patterns.

Tericia's voice crackles over the radio. "Opening the second wormhole now."

A moment passes. Then, before them, a rift tears open again, smooth and brilliant. The planet appears on the other side—large, tinted red by the giant red star in the system, patches of land and water.

The entire crew stares.

"Holy shit," Nick whispers. "That's not just a planet. That's a world."

Neither ship moves. Everyone watches in stunned silence.

"It's... beautiful," Lester finally says. "We've only ever had artist renderings of planets near a red star. This is next level."

They inch forward, both vessels drifting through the wormhole.

As the last meter of their ships clears the wormhole's edge, the portal collapses behind them.

They are here now. Truly here. A new world.

No way back unless everything works perfectly.

'I hope I can get us home,' Tericia thinks as she adjusts her display. But she says nothing.

Nobody does. The view silences them.

An ocean gleams beneath an alien sun. Cloud patterns swirl. Massive continents stretch across the globe. Forests? Ice? It's impossible to tell yet if this planet is habitable.

Parmen finally breaks the silence. "Maybe we should scan something. You know… send a probe?"

"Yes," Tericia says, voice faint. She's still awestruck. "Good idea."

She presses a series of commands and releases a probe. It detaches, tumbles for a moment, then stabilizes as it approaches the atmosphere of this planet, and begins transmitting.

They watch.

Hope swelling in their chests.

Waiting for the world to answer.

CHAPTER 18

Tericia, Lester, Nick and his family, and Parmen stand together in stunned silence, surrounded by the ruins of an abandoned city. Skyscrapers—once proud spires of a civilization lost to time—loom overhead, their facades faded to dull gray beneath the planet's hauntingly red star. The probe they had deployed revealed a planet that was not just habitable, but one that had once pulsed with intelligent life. Yet now, it lay silent.

No birds. No movement. Just the crunch of gravel beneath their boots and the gentle sound of wind moving through the area.

"Anyone?" Lester breaks the silence, squinting up at the empty buildings that seem to watch them back.

"Anyone… what?" Tericia asks, her eyes narrowing as she scans the horizon. "Anyone here? Anyone know what's going on? Anyone understand how a place so alive could suddenly be so still? Anyone have answers? Because we've got a million damn questions. No answers to any of them."

Parmen takes a step forward, then another, his boots scraping against cracked pavement as he turns toward a half-collapsed building. "Answers are where you look," he says flatly. "Let's go find some."

He doesn't wait for agreement. He just walks. Determined. Maybe to distract himself from the lingering trauma of being left behind. Maybe to claim a purpose before someone else does.

Lester and Tericia exchange a glance. He shrugs; she nods. And they follow.

Nick, who had been scanning the opposite direction while holding his youngest daughter's hand, turns sharply to see them moving. "Hey! Wait up," he calls, motioning to his wife and children. "Stick close. No idea what's out here."

The air is breathable, gravity stable, and the ambient temperature hovers at a comfortable level. Yet the red tint of the sky and the strange stillness make Earth feel a million years away.

The building they approach looks eerily familiar— something like a multi-unit dwelling, or perhaps an apartment complex. Its clean lines and use of glass and alloy are uncannily human.

"How is this even possible?" Tericia murmurs, brushing her fingers across the cold surface of a doorframe. "This architecture... it's like Earth. Exactly like Earth, yet just different enough to know better."

"Parallel evolution?" Lester suggests half-heartedly.

"Or someone has been here before," Nick adds darkly.

Parmen spins around, pulling a set of tiny comm tabs from his utility vest. "We're splitting up. Let's cover more ground. These work within a ten-kilometer radius. Keep them on. Say something if you find something."

They each take one, fitting them snugly over their ears. Parmen tests his channel, muttering something about protocol before breaking into a full sprint down the road, disappearing behind a crumbling monument.

"Where the hell is he going?" Tericia calls after him.

"Scouting," he replies over comms, breathless but amused. "I've got legs and training. I can move fast. I'll check buildings over there. I'd give you a direction or a quadrant but we don't have a system setup for this place yet."

Tericia shakes her head with a smirk. "Of course you will."

Nick gestures toward a squat building with wide doors and weathered signage. "That looks like a storefront. Maybe we'll find supplies—or records, maybe even tech."

"Should we split up too?" Tericia asks, glancing toward Lester.

"Hell no. You think I want to die alone on an alien planet? I'm staying with you," he says, tossing her a wink that tugs a reluctant smile from her lips.

They approach the front of the structure. The door, surprisingly, is not sealed. A faint flicker of movement inside catches Tericia's attention. The shifting of a shadow that isn't normal. Her body tenses.

"Did you see that?" she whispers.

Lester nods slowly. "Something moved. Could be an animal. Or..." he trails off.

They freeze, listening. Watching. Something shifts again, this time unmistakably—a shape moving in the dimness behind the cracked glass of a window. Deliberate movement.

"Could be automated tech. Could be... something else," Lester says, still trying to think of something less scary than what he really thinks it is, death in alien form.

Should they go inside? Should they wait? Should they run? Inform the others over coms? They don't get a chance to debate it. They don't get to decide. The decision is made for them.

The door creaks open.

Both Lester and Tericia instinctively reach out, placing protective hands in front of one another, each trying to shield the other. Pushing themselves backward, out of harm's way. They slowly retreat a step, bracing for whatever might emerge.

Out steps a man. A human man.

He gasps in shock at seeing them, his hand shooting to his chest like he's just been punched in the sternum. His breath catches, gray-blue eyes wide with disbelief as they dart between the two strangers. His posture is startled but not aggressive—more confusion than threat.

He's lean, lanky even, with the sort of wiry build born of long days in labs and rugged missions rather than any formal military discipline. His dark brown curls are overgrown and tangled, falling around a face that looks like it hasn't seen a mirror in days. A patchy scruff covers his jaw, and his field jacket hangs slightly off his frame, too big for him, battered and streaked with dust, the Borvil insignia all but scraped away from wear. His boots, that don't seem to fit him right, are stained, soles worn thin—proof he's been walking for a while, or wearing someone else's clothes.

He fumbles at his hip, reaching for something—probably a weapon—but the motion is clumsy, uncertain, like someone doing what they think they're supposed to do. It's clear he's not used to violence.

"Stop!" Tericia blurts, thrusting her hand forward, palm out. "There's no need for that!"

The man hesitates, hand hovering near a worn holster, fingers twitching with indecision. He squints at them, still not lowering his guard completely, but his body language shifts—relieved, curious.

Lester narrows his eyes, breathing heavily. "Who are you?"

The man freezes. "How?" he asks, still panting. "How are you here? How did you—humans? Here? Language?"

"Who are you?" Tericia asks cautiously, seeing that the man wasn't expecting anyone else. "Did you come from Earth?"

"Umm... yeah... umm... My name's Kleom," he says, still trying to catch his breath. "Yeah. Earth. Borvil sent me out here on a recon assignment. I've been stranded for days."

"Stranded?" Lester echoes. "Let me guess—wormhole? No return trip?"

"Exactly that. They didn't tell us it was one way." Kleom's voice tightens with resentment. "I mean, they said they would open the wormhole again after a week, but it feels like abandonment."

"Those bastards," Lester growls. "They keep pulling this shit."

Kleom looks at Lester with a look of confusion, still unsure what he is seeing.

"Did you use the same wormhole device to get here? Use the same one twice?" Tericia asks, trying to piece together the puzzle.

"Yes. Once to a binary star system located five thousand nine hundred and eleven light years from Earth, and then from there to this planet," Kleom replies. "They told us to keep going through until we find something important. Up to eleven times."

"And did they tell you how they were going to retrieve you?" Tericia asks.

"And what do you mean by us?" Lester asks.

"They are going to post a wormhole device at each entry to open it up after one week," Kleom shares, a hint of doubt seeping through his now calm façade.

"Kleom," Lester says, stepping closer. "You said 'us.' Who else is with you?"

"My military escort. Gestwell," Kleom reveals. "Total asshole. Haven't seen him in hours. Figured he went back to the ship or wandered off."

"Found him!" Parmen's voice crackles through the comms, laced with tension.

Lester and Tericia spin around just in time to see Parmen being pushed forward at gunpoint.

Gestwell steps into view, weapon raised, eyes hard. "I'm under orders to kill you on sight," he announces, pressing a boot to Parmen's back and shoving him to the ground. "Your faces are on my kill list. No exceptions."

"Then why haven't you pulled the trigger yet?" Tericia asks, stepping forward, hands up, eyes fixed.

"Because I don't know what you're capable of," Gestwell says. "And because we're all stuck here. But don't worry— once I get a ride home, I'll take care of you."

"That's the dumbest plan I've ever heard," Lester says. "You really think they'll let you live after this? After seeing us? Even if you kill us, you already know too much. I think you should hand over your weapons, work with us, and turn on Borvil."

"How do you know we work for… Oh. Kleom talked, didn't he? Idiot," Gestwell says, looking at Kleom with eyes of disapproval.

"I'm a scientist asshole. I am curious and want answers. Not deception," Kleom replies.

"Anyway, they promised extraction," Gestwell snaps. "And until I get it, you are now my hostages. Barter for going home."

"Are you really that naïve?" Tericia asks. "After everything you've seen from them?"

Before Gestwell can answer, Nick steps into view behind him, weapon drawn. "Drop it. Now."

Gestwell turns, but it's too late. Parmen uses the distraction to twist under him, yanking Gestwell's leg hard enough to snap it. There's a sickening pop. The soldier goes down hard. Parmen's on top of him before he hits the ground, disarming him in one motion.

Gestwell screams, flailing. Parmen ends it with a swift blow to the temple. The man goes limp.

"We need to get him to a hospital," Tericia says quickly, assessing the damage. "He's not going to walk again anytime soon."

"How exactly do you propose we do that?" Kleom asks, clearly skeptical.

Tericia smiles slyly. "Well, I'm happy to hear that Borvil wasn't paying attention to our last iteration of the device changes and didn't implement those modifications on all of their copies. Gives us an advantage."

"Did they really make a dozen of them?" Lester asks, calculating that is what would be needed for the number of wormhole openings Kleom is allowed.

"We don't take chances!" Tericia says in a mocking tone, trying to emulate Tems and his annoying voice. "Plus, they gave us one of the backups to save Parmen," Tericia says in her normal voice.

"Wait," Kleom says slowly, realization dawning. "You two... You're the engineers who built these devices."

"Yes," Tericia says. "And we're going to destroy every last one that Borvil has. They can't and should never have the power that comes with this technology."

"There is one easy..." Lester starts.

"NO! We aren't doing that!" Tericia interrupts.

"Easy what?" Kleom asks with intrigue.

"Forget it. Just tell us where the devices are kept," Tericia demands, changing the subject.

"I don't know. They just gave us a ship and told us to go," Kleom states, clearly not high enough in command to know anything.

"Fuck. Well, I guess we need to get some answers," Tericia says, clearly ready to challenge Kleom. "Kleom, you have a choice. Join us and put Borvil in your rearview mirror or stay here and wait for them, probably meeting your own death once they knew we were here," Tericia states.

"It's hard to answer that. I mean, look where we are. Proof of alien life. A different world. I could stay here for years, exploring," Kleom says with excitement. "I mean, don't get me wrong, Borvil is evil and has been a pain in my ass, but this…" Kleom puts his hands out, pointing to everything, looking around, with a giant smile on his face.

"Yes. I couldn't agree more with all of that. This is the biggest discovery in human existence," Tericia states plainly.

"I want credit! I saw it first!" Parmen blurts out, raising his hand.

"You will. If we live long enough and clear our names," Lester replies.

"Oh, yeah. That," Parmen replies, lowering his head, a small smile forming on his face as if he was part of an inside joke.

"You're going to die before this is over, Kleom. They will either leave you here to die or will kill you to take all credit just to keep you silent as to what you have seen," Tericia says bluntly.

Kleom's eyes go wide in disbelief before dropping his head with the realization that Tericia is correct.

"Listen. Maybe we can work something out. Leave me here with some protection, some weapons maybe. I don't know. Let me explore and figure things out here. You go fight whatever fight is needed," Kleom requests.

"I'd like to stay too," Lester shares. "Science and exploration are my favorite!"

"Well, before I say yes to anyone, do any of you have access to food and water?" Terica asks everyone.

They all sort of just stare at each other and start looking around.

"Thought so. Looks like our first order of business is to get supplies here for a basecamp situation," Tericia says. "And I know just the place to get everything we need. But, before we do that, we need to drop Gestwell at a hospital, and I have an idea on how to make this device even smaller and more maneuverable. Let's get to work."

CHAPTER 19

A wormhole pulses to life with its familiar hum, its outer rim shimmering like liquid glass. On the other side, not the stars, not open space—but a long, narrow corridor. Shadowy. Damp. Thick with dust and webbing so old it seems to sag under its own weight.

"Where is that?" Lester asks, peering through the distortion as if trying to push the shadows back with his gaze.

"That," Tericia replies, her voice quiet but rich with memory, "is an old subterranean bunker. Built before the end of the War of Madness. The elites—politicians, corporate execs, anyone with power—they built these places to outlast the chaos. Some used them. Most didn't. Many of the richest were killed before they could even enter."

She takes a few steps toward the portal, as though drawn in by the past itself. "There was one group—called themselves the Society of Survivors. They pooled resources to build a network of bunkers, one for each major family line. But the elites wanted it. So, they slaughtered the Society—only to realize afterward that no one knew the locations. It was never found... until now."

Kleom folds his arms, incredulously. "Then how the hell do you know where it is?"

A smirk flickers across Tericia's lips. "My great-grandmother left breadcrumbs. In her diary, encoded. Took me years to make sense of it. But the family's always had this odd tradition—encrypting messages using the street number of our original home. It was subtle. Smart. Worked for generations."

Lester raises an eyebrow. "You still use that code?"

"I do. Which is why I'm not sharing it with anyone," she answers, deadpan. "Not even you."

Kleom tilts his head. "So what—you think this place still has viable supplies after all this time?"

"I don't hope. I know," she says, gripping Holepunch like a lifeline. "The Society planned to be down here for decades. They were over-prepared. Now, we find out if their paranoia pays off."

Before anyone else can speak, Parmen's boots thud past them. Without a word, he steps through the wormhole, landing with a quiet grunt inside the bunker. "Less talking," he calls back. "More doing."

Tericia grins faintly and follows, stepping into the dark unknown. One by one, the others jump through, the wormhole closing behind them like a whisper. Darkness swallows them whole.

"Anyone bring a flashlight?" Lester mutters, shifting his feet in the sudden void.

Parmen answers with a rustle of fabric. From a pouch strapped to his thigh, he pulls out a handful of tiny spheres—light bugs. He tosses them across the floor. They skitter away, self-righting as they go, then each bursts to life with a soft glow. The corridor ahead blooms in fragments—dim pools of pale blue light stretching into shadows.

Their small group advances cautiously, boots brushing through dust that has settled for generations. They check each room as the go, peer through each door. Every one they pass yields more of the same—bunk rooms, beds untouched; storage lockers long emptied or never filled; bathrooms dry and barren. The silence of the place feels almost sacred, like they've trespassed into a forgotten tomb.

Eventually, they find a stairwell. Rusted but intact. Parmen tosses another cluster of light bugs down the spiral, watching them bounce and spiral into the darkness.

"Three levels," he reports, peering over the edge. "We've got a lot of ground to cover."

Tericia steps forward, her tone firm. "Parmen, you take the lowest floor. Take Kleom with you. Check for generators, wiring, anything that looks like it might power this place up."

Parmen nods and immediately starts downward. "On it."

"Kleom—move!" Tericia adds, pointing after him.

"I'm going! Damn," Kleom mutters as he follows, his footsteps echoing behind.

"Lester and I will check the mid-level. Nick," she turns to him, "get your family settled. Find a few rooms, check for anything resembling safety or comfort."

Nick salutes half-seriously and turns to his wife and kids. "Alright, come on."

As the others disappear down their respective corridors, Lester and Tericia begin opening doors along their floor.

Dust motes dance in the air. Every room feels haunted by absence—worn couches frozen in time, dining tables set for meals that never came.

"So, what are we really doing, Tericia?" Lester finally asks, breaking the quiet.

Tericia stops at a sealed door and leans her forehead against it, exhaling slowly. "Looking for supplies. Weapons. Water. Food. Anything to make that planet livable. Or here. Maybe both. We need backup plans. We need to make this place a fallback—something we can return to if it all goes to hell."

"That's not what I meant." Lester's voice drops. "What's the real plan? Are we explorers? Rebels? Refugees? Are we running… or going on the offensive?"

She turns to him, eyes heavy with the weight of everything. "Yes. All of the above."

They find a kitchen, faded and silent. Tericia tosses down a few light bugs. The faint glow reveals shelves, utensils, pots and pans still in place. But the overheads remain stubbornly dark.

"I really hope Parmen finds the power soon," Tericia says, opening cupboards.

As if summoned, the hallway lights flicker once—twice— then stay on, humming to life with a steady buzz. Tericia lets out a genuine smile and turns to Lester.

"Looks like he did it," Lester says, chuckling as he heads toward the door. "Let me get the kitchen lights."

He finds the control panel crusted over with layers of dust and age-old paint. With a grunt, he heads back inside, grabs a kitchen knife, and begins scraping at the seams. Focused. Determined.

"Whatcha doin'?" comes Parmen's voice out of nowhere.

Lester jumps like he's been electrocuted. Knife raised. "Damn it, Parmen! Don't sneak up on people like that!"

"Easy now, Lester. It was a joke," Parmen says, holding his hands in front of him, easing the situation.

"Just trying to get to the manual switch. Motion isn't working," Lester says through heavy breathing. "And don't just jump out at people who aren't ready for it."

Parmen laughs, casually takes the knife, and pries open the panel. A flick of the switch—and the kitchen bursts into full light. Rows of shelves and drawers now clearly visible, lined with cans, dried goods, dishware. Not just intact—but immaculate, despite the dust.

"Oh, hell yes," Tericia says. "Score."

Elsewhere in the bunker, the team continues to explore. Cabinets full of preserved food. Lockers of emergency gear. Even ancient medical kits, sealed in vacuum-tight packs.

Back in the kitchen, Lester leans against the counter, tension tightening his features.

"We're in a bad place," he says finally.

Tericia doesn't look up. "How so?"

"They've got more devices. At least ten. Maybe more. Somewhere, someone's figuring out how to improve them. And if they get there first, if they find us first, if they own the tech before we're ready... we're screwed."

Tericia closes a cupboard and turns to him, calm but resolved. "Then we don't let that happen. We get Nick's family settled, less baggage to worry about. We secure this base. And then we go hunting."

"And if it all goes sideways?"

She freezes. Her eyes flick to his. Then harden. "We're not talking about that. Ever."

Lester opens his mouth to protest—but she cuts him off with a kiss. A brief one, charged with desperation and defiance.

"Not now," she whispers.

Parmen reappears in the doorway, knocking on the frame, everyone else standing out in the hallway. "We good? Let's keep moving."

"Wait," Lester says. "We can't keep aimlessly poking around. We need priorities. There's a new world waiting. A planet. The greatest discovery in history. What the hell are we doing in some dusty bunker that appears to be a dead end?"

He spins to face them all. "Tell me I'm wrong."

Tericia pauses, looking at the floor for a long beat. "You're not. But survival still comes first."

"We have wormholes!" Lester exclaims. "We have the means to go anywhere. Anytime."

"I say we go back to the planet," Kleom throws in.

"I say we prep here first," Nick says. "My family comes first. Then I'm with you."

"Until we've got food, water, and shelter, we don't have anything," Tericia says, her tone final. "We build the foundation first. Here. Now. Then we make our move. We have some food, maybe edible, no water, and this place is hardly livable yet."

Everyone nods slowly. The gravity of it settling in.

Lester sighs. "Fine. But the clock's ticking. Let's get this place livable."

Tericia steps aside and gestures toward the next room. "Then let's not waste any more time."

CHAPTER 20

Tericia crouches beside a rusted, long-dormant mechanical unit in the far corner of the subterranean facility's lowest level. She wipes grime from the faded label and squints to read the partially obscured wording: WATER SUPPLY REGULATOR – PRIMARY PUMP. With the butt of her palm, she knocks gently against the casing. The metal vibrates faintly, but no life stirs within it.

"Looks like we need to fix this," she mutters, wiping her hand on her pants, "and then we're in business. At least when it comes to water."

Beside her, Parmen inspects a network of corroded pipes running along the concrete wall. His eyes trace the lines, assessing for damage. "Yeah. Looks like water's at the core of everything down here—long-term power, sanitation, maybe even climate control. If we restore flow and pressure, we get the whole place breathing again. Assuming there aren't any catastrophic leaks, of course."

Tericia exhales and leans back against the wall, thinking. "Hmmm..."

Parmen glances at her, eyebrows raised. "What?"

"I'm just thinking," she replies, her gaze distant. "Wondering if this is really the best place for us. I mean, it's potentially functional, but... maybe there's something better. Somewhere more modern, more equipped."

Parmen chuckles softly, his voice echoing faintly off the concrete walls. "No chance. This bunker's off-grid, untouched by modern surveillance. You go topside, even for a minute, and Borvil will have eyes on you. You know how they operate. They've embedded themselves in every corner of tech. 'We don't take chances.' They should really make that their moniker."

His voice mimics Tems's now-infamous catchphrase with just the right amount of venom.

"They've used their position to manipulate governments, private industries, even research institutions. No, down here? We're invisible. And that's our advantage."

Tericia tilts her head toward him, her lips twitching at his impression. "So, finally, you're fully on our side now?"

"Yeah," Parmen replies, the smile fading as his tone deepens. "Lester told me what happened to you in the lab. That's not war. That's a slaughterhouse wearing a lab coat. That's something else entirely."

"Fucked up doesn't even cover it," Tericia says quietly, her voice tight. "I still wake up some nights with their faces. Every person we lost. Every one of them... I recruited. I believed in this dream, and they believed in me."

Parmen reaches out, placing a steady hand on her shoulder. "You didn't kill them. You gave them purpose. They made their choices. You didn't know what Borvil was going to do."

He hesitates, turning away. "I've lost people too—soldiers under my command. Some because I gave the wrong order. Some because I hesitated. Some... because the mission didn't give a fuck who made it back. I carry that weight, too."

Tericia sees the mist in his eyes just as he turns and starts walking out of the room.

"I do know what you mean," she says gently, her voice following him. "Thank you. Now let's get what we need to fix this system. One step at a time."

"Everyone know what they're looking for?" Tericia asks, her voice brisk, as she finishes keying the coordinates into Holepunch. The glow of the interface casts faint shadows across their faces in the dim light of the bunker's common room.

Lester crosses his arms. "So, we're just robbing stores now? This is our life?"

"Do you have credits? Because I don't," Tericia replies without looking up. "Haven't been paid in ten years. Pretty sure the world thinks we're dead. Pretty sure Borvil prefers it that way."

"We'll need to fix that eventually," Lester says with a sigh.

"We will. When we're ready, we'll tell the world what really happened. All of it. If we survive long enough to do it right," Tericia says, her tone sharp with conviction.

Parmen steps forward, impatient. "Can we just get on with it?"

Tericia nods and taps the final sequence. A blue-white ripple tears into reality, revealing the quiet back aisle of a hardware store. Lights glow overhead. Shelves are stacked with tools, wiring, plumbing supplies.

Nick, Lester, Parmen, and Kleom move quickly through the wormhole.

"You've got ten minutes," Tericia says before the wormhole snaps closed behind them. "Grab what you need. I'll reopen when the timer hits zero."

Inside the store, the four men scatter like professionals executing a heist.

"Keep it low-key. Look like you belong," Parmen mutters. "Don't ask for directions. Don't talk to employees. Just move."

Lester moves with nervous energy, gripping his list as if it might disintegrate. The last time he was outside, he'd been nearly captured—or worse. He finds the plumbing aisle, his eyes darting between part numbers and diagrams. Piping. Couplings. Tools. PipePixies, small robots that do most of the work in hard-to-reach places. He double-checks everything, his pulse quickening.

He senses eyes on him. Two employees, whispering, checking their tablets. Their stares bounce between him and their screens.

Shit.

Lester turns and walks fast. Not running. Not yet.

He rounds the corner and spots Parmen. Relief floods through him.

Then he hears the voices—security guards calling for backup. Employees backing away. More uniforms appear from the front of the store, corralling the area like wolves herding prey, yet trying to stay hidden.

"What's going on?" Parmen asks, voice low.

"I don't know. I think they've ID'd me," Lester replies, clutching his supplies.

"We wait for the wormhole," Parmen says calmly, shifting subtly to place himself between Lester and the incoming guards.

Nick and Kleom reappear, loaded with gear. They freeze at the sight of the encroaching security.

A guard raises his voice. "Step away from that man!"

"Which man?" Parmen smirks. "We're all ruggedly handsome here."

"He's wanted for treason! Armed theft of military assets. He's all over the news!" the guard barks.

Parmen turns to Lester with a raised eyebrow. "Huh. You really made a name for yourself."

"Thirty seconds," Kleom whispers.

More security floods in. Then, with a shatter of glass and a cascade of sparks, soldiers descend from a rooftop skylight, their boots hitting the ground with trained precision.

"Freeze!" one shouts. "On the ground!"

"Ten seconds," Kleom mutters.

Lester can't breathe. His chest tightens. His palms are slick. He can't move. A lot can happen in ten seconds.

"Get ready," Parmen says, eyes on the swirling air behind them. "Don't move until I say."

"Five seconds…"

The smell of ozone curls into the air like burning metal. The temperature shifts.

"Parmen! Move!" Nick yells.

Parmen leaps backward just as the wormhole erupts open behind him. A shimmering ring of salvation.

"Now!" Parmen shouts.

He shoves Lester through first, then pulls Nick and Kleom with him. He grabs his supplies and takes one last look at the chaos before diving through.

The wormhole vanishes behind him with a deafening snap of displaced air, leaving behind only baffled soldiers, guards, and store clerks, blinking at empty space where a fugitive, and three other men had just been.

CHAPTER 21

"That was close," Parmen says between ragged breaths, his expression displaying a strange mix of adrenaline and amusement, like someone who just stepped off a thrill ride and immediately wanted to get back in line.

"Too close," Lester mutters, his voice tight with anxiety. "And I've been labeled a traitor now? A traitor?" He paces a few feet before turning back to face the others. "I've spent my life trying to build something that helps humanity. And now I'm a criminal?"

"We'll fix it," Tericia says, scanning over the crates and armfuls of supplies they've just stolen. "But right now, we need to—"

Kleom collapses.

The sound of his body hitting the floor is sharp and final. Everyone spins around.

He's pale. His breathing shallow and erratic. His limbs twitch as if rebelling against something unseen.

"Shit," Parmen breathes and drops to his knees beside him. He presses two fingers to Kleom's neck, then shifts quickly, applying pressure to a wound near the ribcage. "I thought that snap sounded different."

"What snap?" Tericia demands, already crouching on the other side.

"When the wormhole closed. I heard a sharp pop—thought it was just the energy flux collapsing. But now I realize it was a tracker round. They hit him. There's a tracker inside him. And, unfortunately, it seems they hit something vital."

"Fuck that," Tericia says, already standing. "Cut it out. I'll drop it somewhere else. Somewhere they'll chase it and waste their time."

"Cut...?" Kleom tries to speak, his voice barely more than a breath.

"There's a med-bay," Tericia says. "There's equipment. Might be enough."

"Was there a stretcher?" Parmen asks, never breaking rhythm as he keeps pressure on Kleom's side.

"A gurney," Tericia replies.

"I'm on it!" Nick shouts and bolts from the room.

"You don't even know where it is!" Tericia calls out, groaning, and taking off after him.

They sprint down the corridor, Tericia quickly overtaking Nick and leading them up the stairwell. Her boots echo through the silence like a metronome counting down someone's final seconds.

She rounds the corner, throws open an old, dusty door and reveals a dim, sterile room with a folded gurney in the corner.

"Found the gurney," she says. "Looks like they didn't want to be reminded of their own mortality—kept this room tucked away like an afterthought."

Nick and Tericia grab the gurney, and they wheel it back as carefully as they can.

"Watch the steps," Tericia warns. "We don't need more injuries."

They descend with purpose, their faces tense. When they arrive, they find the others not working, not panicking—but standing in silence.

Parmen is no longer applying pressure. Instead, he's holding a small, blood-slick device in his palm. A tracker. Kleom lies still. Too still.

"What happened?" Tericia asks, her voice hollow.

Parmen doesn't look up. "It was lodged too deep. It hit his lung. He drowned in his own..."

"I get it," she cuts in, not needing the details. Her eyes drop to Kleom's lifeless body for just a second before she steps forward and snatches the tracker from Parmen's hand.

Without a word, she walks to Holepunch and starts inputting coordinates. Her movements are sharp, focused. Cold with purpose.

"Where are you putting it?" Lester asks, his voice quieter now.

"I'm delivering it to the real traitor," Tericia says, her fingers dancing over the interface.

"But... Tems is dead," Lester replies, confused.

"He was never the real one," Tericia says, not looking up. "Tems was a child pretending to be a king. Desperate to earn his father's approval, desperate to mean something. But the one pulling the strings—the one who probably orchestrated all of it—is still breathing."

Lester blinks. "Who?"

"Giles Elliot Borvil," she spits the name like it burns. "The CEO. Tems was just a blunt instrument. Giles is the hand that swung it. He built this empire on manipulation and fear, and he won't stop until he owns the stars. I'm going to make sure he sees how that ends."

A wormhole begins to form, shimmering to life with a low pulse. Tericia lifts the tracker, holding it just inside the vortex as she speaks.

"You can't just portal-hop your way to him," Lester warns. "We don't have the fuel."

"How many jumps left?" she asks.

"Two," he replies. "Two after this one."

"Perfect." She says as she continues to hold the tracker on the other side of the portal, far away from the bunker. "I'm going through. Open this same spot in an hour. After that, we can go get fuel."

"You're going through?" Lester says, incredulous.

"Yes. I'm delivering a message, and if I time it right, I'll have front-row seats to the chaos. Open this location again in one hour."

"We should refuel first," Lester insists.

"Every second that tracker is here is a second closer to discovery," she replies. "And besides…" she smirks faintly, holding up her palm. "I've got the motivation. The rage. That moment of perfect courage where I don't give a damn what happens to me. I'd rather not lose it."

"You're sure?" Parmen asks. "You're walking into the lion's den."

"No," Tericia says with a smirk, stepping through the wormhole. "I'm dragging a ticking bomb into his bedroom. Just remember. One hour. Same spot."

And with that, she steps through and vanishes as the wormhole closes, leaving the others in silence.

CHAPTER 22

Tericia stands alone in Giles Borvil's opulent family estate, the eerie silence pressing in like a second skin. The grandeur of the place, the towering ceilings and polished floors, clash violently with the grime under her nails and the dried blood staining her palm—Kleom's blood. She stares down at the small tracking device resting in her hand.

Without a word, she crosses the bedroom to the enormous bed and lays the tracker gently on a silk pillow, its crimson smear already soaking into the fabric. "Where are you?" she mutters under her breath, heading into the ensuite bathroom.

She turns on the faucet, and cold water sputters from the tap. She thrusts her hands beneath it and begins scrubbing frantically. Red swirls into the sink basin, disappearing down the drain like a secret. She lifts her eyes to the mirror and catches her own reflection—drawn, exhausted, older than she remembers. A survivor, maybe, but at what cost?

"You're not going to find him here," comes a voice—calm, cold, unmistakably familiar.

She spins, breath caught in her throat.

Tems steps into view, as smug and self-satisfied as ever. His suit is sharp, his posture arrogant. But his eyes are cold coals, glowing with malice. A new scar sliding across his face, his only imperfection.

"You're alive…" Tericia's voice barely carries the words. Her body goes rigid with disbelief. "How?"

"Reinforced desk," Tems replies, pacing into the room like he owns it. "The explosive you tossed landed behind me. I vaulted over just in time. Daddy dearest always thought someone might try to kill me. You weren't the first. The desk was… custom." He smirks. "I have to admit, your attempt was impressive. But now it's going to cost you."

He draws a sleek handgun from inside his coat, leveling it with professional ease. Tericia flinches, eyes squeezing shut, waiting for the shot—Tems never hesitates.

But nothing comes.

"Open your eyes, bitch," Tems growls. "I'm not going to kill you… yet."

Her eyes open slowly, the muzzle of the gun still fixed on her chest.

"When are they coming back for you?" he asks.

"In an hour," she answers, voice trembling.

"Then don't expect anyone to interrupt us until then," he snaps, walking over to the pillow and lifting the tracker into his gloved hand. He looks at it, then casually drops the tracker to the marble floor and brings down his boot. It cracks underfoot with a sharp crunch.

"Walk."

He gestures with the gun. Tericia turns, every muscle tight, every nerve on edge. He nudges her out of the bathroom, through the bedroom, and into the grand hallway.

"Call off the attack," Tems says aloud, seemingly to no one.

Tericia stops walking, her eyes catching the discreet earpiece tucked into his right ear. A direct line. Of course.

"Don't stop now," Tems barks. "Move!"

She keeps walking, glancing back. "So that's how far your reach goes... You're not just Borvil's dog anymore. You're plugged into the government."

"The government is just a toy chest for the rich," Tems replies. "Pawns pretending they have power while we move the real pieces. You of all people should've figured that out."

They reach the main staircase.

"You do know they'll open the wormhole right into your father's bedroom," she says, dryly.

"I figured," Tems shrugs. "But we have time. I'm going to make this next hour the worst of your miserable life."

"I've already lived through hell," Tericia snaps. "We could've finished the project eight or nine years ago if you hadn't murdered half the team."

Tems laughs as they descend the staircase.

"I don't give a fuck," he sneers. "If they couldn't perform, they didn't deserve to live. Weakness deserves no reward."

Tericia turns halfway down the stairs and faces him. "And you? Still just daddy's disappointment with a vendetta? Still desperate for approval from a man who will never respect you?"

Tems, towering one step above her, lashes out. His boot drives into her solar plexus. The impact robs her of breath and balance. She crumples, gasping, tumbling down the final steps, crashing onto the marble below with a sickening thud.

He descends slowly, savoring each step.

"You're making this too easy," he says, grinning down at her broken form. "Try to last at least five minutes. Make it interesting."

She groans, trying to push herself up. Blood drips from her lip.

"No," she croaks.

Still able to speak.

Tems corrects that with a savage punch to her face. Her head snaps sideways, teeth clatter to the floor. Blood pools in her mouth.

"Two teeth? Pathetic," Tems scoffs. "Usually I get four with the first hit."

Tericia, defiant even now, spits blood at his feet. "Fuck you," she mumbles.

He grabs her hair and begins dragging her through the halls. Her good hand clutches his wrist, trying to minimize the pain. He hauls her into a new room—dark, cold, sterile. Metal racks line the walls. A torture chamber.

"Standard issue for my family," Tems says with pride, pushing her against a vertical steel slab. The restraints close around her limbs with a hiss. He steps back, admiring his work.

"That was only five minutes," he says with a devilish smile. "I can't wait to see what happens with the rest of our time together."

Time slips into madness.

One by one, her fingernails are torn free. The pain is white-hot, numbing, a flood of agony so intense it barely registers anymore. Her voice is hoarse, raw from screams. Blood drips onto the metal floor.

Tems circles her like a predator. "Just tell me how to dial locations. Why make this harder than it has to be?"

Tericia lifts her head, her eyes hollow but defiant, and through every labored breath, she responds. "You… shouldn't… have… that… much… power."

Tems roars with frustration. "I already do! I just need reach! Across the stars, from anywhere! To anywhere. With that tech, I'll surpass my father. I'll take everything that should have been mine years ago!"

Tericia's head tilts upward, forcing eye contact. "I bet he'd be… so proud of you now."

Tems freezes. The hatred on his face is no longer restrained. His hand goes to his gun.

"I was going to let you say goodbye to your crew," he snarls. "Let you watch while I shoot each of them in the head. But now? They'll just have to find your corpse."

He raises the weapon.

"Freeze!"

Parmen's voice cuts through the tension like a blade. He stands in the doorway, weapon trained on Tems.

Tems doesn't hesitate—he slams his palm to his chest. A hidden tether snaps taut and yanks him backward into a concealed panel in the wall. The moment is gone in a blink.

"Fuck!" Parmen shouts, then bolts into the room. "Get her free. Now!"

Nick and Lester rush to the restraints, working furiously. Parmen holds his gun, eyes scanning every corner of the room.

"You're early," Tericia whispers to Lester as he cradles her head.

"I got impatient," Lester replies, voice cracking as tears spill down his cheeks. "Something told me you needed us sooner."

"Less talking, more moving!" Parmen barks.

They lift Tericia from the table. Her body is battered, bloodied, barely responsive. Her strength is gone, but her spirit still lingers behind her eyes.

They make their way back upstairs, every step a struggle. But eventually they reach the bedroom.

"No sign of Tems. Hopefully he is sitting in an escape room, waiting for us to leave." Parmen mutters. "Get her through. Now."

They carry her through the wormhole.

And then they close it—locking the darkness behind them.

CHAPTER 23

"She's stable. Just needs to recover," Nick says, his voice quiet, as if afraid louder words might break something fragile in the room. "The machine should do its thing and fix her up. It'll take time, though—not as fast as modern systems. If we had more fuel, I'd suggest a proper hospital."

"We'll make getting fuel our next step," Lester replies, arms crossed tightly over his chest. His eyes don't leave Tericia as she lies on the medical bed, bruised, bandaged, and barely conscious. "It's either fuel or we never use this device again. We still don't even know how to get out of this damn bunker."

"I know how I'm getting out," a voice interrupts, laced with venom and confidence.

Everyone's attention snaps toward the doorway. Standing there, his silhouette framed by the dim hall light, is Tems. His suit is torn and streaked with blood, but the gun in his hand is steady—pressed against the temple of Nick's wife, Rebecca. Her face is frozen in fear, lips trembling but silent. Her eyes tell Nick everything he needs to know. The kids are safe. Hidden.

"You're going to show me how this device works," Tems growls, his eyes locked on Lester. "You'll open it where I say, and I'll take what's mine."

"Please, just let her go and—"

"And what?" Tems barks, cutting Nick off mid-plea. "Let go of my leverage so your little commando pal can shoot me? No one speaks. No one moves. Except Lester."

Nick's hands hover in the air, unsure whether to rush Tems or collapse. Lester takes a slow, reluctant step forward.

"Lester?" Tems sneers.

Lester nods faintly. His eyes flick to Tericia again—pale and still—and then to Rebecca, whose terror reflects every ounce of his failure to protect the people he loves. His stomach knots. He's been running from this moment since the day they first met Tems. There's no running now.

"I'm waiting," Tems says, tightening his grip on Rebecca's shoulder.

"We don't have enough fuel at this point," Parmen interjects, stepping forward. "One more opening is all we have left. Let us get fuel first, then we can—"

BANG.

Parmen's sentence cuts off. The shot echoes like thunder.

He stumbles backward, eyes wide, blood blooming across his side. He falls hard to his knees, then collapses face-first onto the ground. The room goes silent except for the hum of the life support machine and Nick's strangled gasp.

"I'll find fuel where I'm going," Tems mutters coldly. He jerks Rebecca forward, pushing her roughly toward Nick. "Here. Keep your wife. You've all been such a joy." Tems grabs Lester as he approaches and walks him back to the device. They walk through the door and Tems latches the door behind him, sealing Lester and himself inside the chamber with Holepunch. Alone.

"Walk me through it," he says, aiming his gun squarely at Lester's chest.

Lester obeys. He moves slowly, every gesture precise, controlled—like handling explosives. He shows Tems the modified interface, the way the coordinates are entered now, how to lock in a destination. But inside, Lester's mind races. He's not going to hand this monster the keys to the universe. Not after everything.

"Where do you want to go?" Lester asks, his voice hollow.

"The lab," Tems says, eyes glittering. "Should be easy for you to remember. You and your little girlfriend brought me enough people to paint it red with blood."

Lester nods and enters the coordinates, despite wanting to throw up thinking about his fallen colleagues. His hand hovers over the execute button. He thinks of Tericia—her screams, her broken body. He thinks of Kleom's lifeless eyes. Of Parmen bleeding on the medical room's floor. Of the countless others who never made it out.

Tems sees the hesitation and slams the execute command himself.

The wormhole explodes into life with a crackling shimmer, revealing the familiar sterile corridors of the lab beyond. Tems grabs the device and tries to shove it through, but it jerks to a halt. It's locked in place.

"You need to go through first," Lester says. "The device won't budge unless someone's there to guide it. If it starts to go and you're not in control, it'll tear itself apart." Lester takes a step back and puts up his hands, demonstrating that he isn't trying anything malicious.

Tems eyes him suspiciously but sees no reason to doubt it. He steps through the wormhole, half on one side, half on the other side of the glowing ring. He reaches back and begins pulling on the device. Still no movement.

Frustrated, he braces to pull harder—and that's when Lester makes his move.

With a shaky hand, he reaches toward the side of the device and presses the emergency close button—an unassuming panel that Tericia had insisted they install. A failsafe. One they had been using regularly.

The wormhole collapses with a deafening pop, and Tems's arm and leg drops to the floor.

Blood pools beneath the limbs as Lester stumbles back, staring at the mangled remains. His breath comes in shallow gulps. His limbs shake. His mind spins.

He just tore Tems into pieces. For real this time. "There's no coming back from that. He'll bleed out quickly," Lester says to the empty room.

The device lets out a low warning tone. The fuel is gone. The display flashes red.

Fuel exhausted. Wormhole activity suspended.

He walks slowly to the doorway, opens it, and collapses against the wall in the hallway. The adrenaline fades. Guilt, relief, shock, and pain collide inside him.

He doesn't know how long he sits there. Seconds? Minutes?

Then he bolts upright.

"Tericia," he gasps.

Lester runs back to the medical bay. As he bursts through the door, he freezes.

She's standing. Barely.

Tericia is bracing herself against a medical cabinet, weak and swaying, trying to lift Parmen's limp body onto the bed.

"Help me," she croaks, her voice thin but iron-willed. "This guy's heavy."

Lester rushes to her side, his arms around her before she can protest. Together, they lift Parmen onto the bed. Tericia collapses into Lester's arms.

"What happened?" she asks in whispers.

Lester holds her tighter. "I'll tell you later. After you have recovered."

CHAPTER 24

"The gunshot woke me up," Tericia says, her voice hoarse but steady as she and Lester wrestle Parmen's limp body onto the med-bed. "Turns out death trumps fingernails and missing teeth. Hopefully he still has time. Hopefully he hasn't lost too much blood."

The bed's automated system chirps to life, scanning and stabilizing Parmen's vitals. Tericia leans against the wall, sweat dripping from her brow, her fingers trembling not from weakness, but from adrenaline.

"How was your day?" she asks, sarcasm coating her words like armor as she leans back and sighs from exhaustion.

"Productive," Lester replies, not missing a beat. "I killed Tems."

Tericia raises an eyebrow, offering a tired, crooked smirk. "You did, huh?"

"Yeah. His arm and leg are still by Holepunch. Probably getting blood all over it." Lester's voice shifts—part disbelief, part pride, part horror masked in humor.

While the moment earns a faint exhale of amusement from Tericia, her expression sobers quickly. "That's great and all, but that also means we're officially out of fuel, right?"

"Yeah," Lester admits, rubbing the back of his neck. "That's the downside. But hey, we still have the device—and he doesn't. Borvil doesn't."

Nick's voice cuts in from the doorway, his arm wrapped protectively around his wife and kids. "We want out. We'll take our chances outside."

Tericia doesn't hesitate. "I don't blame you. But unless you found the exit, we're stuck here. No fuel. No coordinates. No wormholes."

Rebecca's face twists with fear. She buries her face in Nick's chest, breaking down. Her last straw, broken. Nick holds her tightly, whispering reassurances even he doesn't fully believe.

"We'll find it," Lester says, trying to inject hope into the room. "This place was built for survival. They wouldn't have made it without a way in or out. We just have to be scientific about it."

Nick's brows draw together. "What do you suggest?"

"Wall sections," Tericia answers, already shifting into mission mode. "Check every wall. Look for inconsistencies. A draft, a seam, something that breaks the pattern. My guess is they disguised the exit to keep morale intact during a fallout. No temptation to run. No constant reminder that there is an outside."

"Split up to do it faster?" Nick asks.

"Definitely not. We need all eyes on each section. Everyone sees something different. What you miss, someone else might catch."

"This room's as good a place to start as any," Lester adds, eyeing the panels with sudden excitement.

"Let's mark them as we go," he continues. "Panel identifiers. Easy to track."

"We don't have time to build a whole system," Tericia says, already pacing the room.

"It's simple! Floor number, first two letters of the room name, then number each panel clockwise from the door. This one's 2ME1," Lester says, standing next to a panel and clearly invigorated.

"And hallways?" Tericia asks, hands on hips.

"Same. Start at the stairs and go clockwise."

Tericia nods. "Alright, genius. Go find something to write on the walls with and start tagging panels. Nick, you and your family find writing surfaces—pads, tablets, journals—whatever we can use for notes."

Nick nods and guides his family out to search. Tericia remains behind, glancing at Parmen as the machine does its work.

The next hour passes in bursts of movement and sharp focus. Lester runs through the halls, tagging panel after panel like a man possessed. Nick and his family return with a stack of scavenged clipboards and digital pads. Tericia checks Parmen every few minutes, watching for any sign of improvement.

By the time they regroup, Lester's face glistens with sweat, but his eyes gleam. "Ready!"

Nick smiles faintly. "Science really gets you going, huh?"

Lester nods. "It's been a long time since I could just… analyze something."

"Then let's proceed," Tericia says, stepping to the first wall panel. "Thirty seconds max. First pass is just about spotting anomalies."

They examine panel after panel, moving room by room, hallway by hallway, floor by floor. They break only for water and brief stretches. Each of them writes down anything they think might be important. The atmosphere lightens with the rhythm of it—some laughter, the occasional joke, even quiet appreciation of the process.

But the exhaustion starts to show. By the time they finish, shoulders sag and legs ache. Three floors. Many rooms. Long hallways. So many panels to analyze.

"All right," Tericia says, sitting on the edge of a nearby crate. "Which panels stood out?"

Lester frowns and scrolls through his notes. "Three anomalies—3HA6, 2HA5, and 1HA4. Each one's an outlier, but here's the weird part: they all match each other. Same material. Same scuffing. Slightly warmer temperature."

Tericia's eyes narrow. "All identical but placed on three different floors? And one section apart from the next."

Lester nods. "Too consistent to be random. But three exit doors? That doesn't make sense."

"Unless…" Tericia says, trailing off, her mind already sprinting toward a conclusion.

Lester and Nick both lean forward.

CHAPTER 25

"It's got to be here somewhere," Tericia mutters, crouched beside a section of wall, one hand brushing the dust away from the faint scuff mark embedded in the metal surface. She taps a finger against it, tracing the shape. "This scratch says everything we need to know. Look at the arc. That's a hinge line. It's curved. Subtle. But it's where the door would swing open, if it ever has."

Lester squints, leaning in. "I believe you. But believing doesn't help if we don't see a mechanism to open it. We've been through this hallway half a dozen times. It's just—wall."

Tericia huffs, ignoring him, already scanning the adjacent surface again. "Control panels? Electrical boxes? Computers? Even a fucking emergency latch would be helpful. Come on, there has to be something."

Nick and his family fan out nearby, his kids peeking into nooks while Rebecca runs a hand over the wall, searching for even the faintest variation in the texture. "It's like a magician's trick," she murmurs. "There's a secret, but we're looking from the wrong angle."

The sound of shuffling interrupts them, followed by a familiar voice—weak, rasping. "What's all the commotion?"

Everyone turns.

"Parmen!" Lester exclaims.

Parmen stands in the hallway, hunched slightly, one arm pressing against his ribs. The place where he'd been shot still bears faint stains on his shirt, though the color has faded from crimson to rust. "What the hell are you doing out of bed?" Tericia demands, marching toward him.

"I was awake. Bored. Figured I'd stretch my legs before they fell off," he mutters, attempting a smirk.

"You shouldn't be on your feet. The machine isn't finished with you yet," she says, her voice somewhere between reprimand and concern. "It said it would take three days to finish."

Parmen offers a weak shrug and leans against the wall, steadying himself with his free hand. "So what's going on? You find something?"

"We are trying to find a way out of this bunker," Nick says without looking back.

"Why not just…"

"Out of fuel," Lester interrupts. "You can thank Tems for that. At least the limbs of his that still lay near Holepunch."

"I might just have to pay my respects," Parmen says and tries to laugh, but the pain winces his focus back to the present moment.

"We think we found the exit," Nick says. "There's a scratch—like a hinge groove—but no control system. No button. No keyhole. Nothing."

Parmen squints down the hall, catching the shimmer of scratched metal beneath the light. "You're sure it's a door?"

"As sure as I can be without it opening it in my face," Tericia replies.

Parmen winces as he pushes off the wall. "Mind if I take a look?"

"Yes. You should be in bed," Tericia says, alarmed, but Parmen waves her off.

"Lying in bed while we're trapped underground isn't exactly a comfort." He moves slowly, each step deliberate, and reaches the edge of the stairs. Then, unexpectedly, he stops.

"Wait... wait," he says, turning slowly and looking up at the low ceiling above the half-landing. He shades his eyes and peers into the shadows above. "Anyone got a light?"

Lester grabs a flashlight from his belt and hands it to Parmen. He raises it carefully, and a panel—barely perceptible—becomes visible. A square, faintly different from the surrounding metal. Slightly raised edges. Painted the same color, maybe even intentionally dirtied to camouflage it.

"There it is," Parmen says with a strained grin. "You'd never spot it unless you were below it, looking up. Clever bastards."

"How do we get to it?" Nick asks, craning his neck.

"Ladder. And someone to climb it who doesn't have a bullet hole or a cracked rib," Parmen grunts.

The group retrieves the sturdiest ladder they can find in the storage room and positions it below the panel. Nick volunteers instantly.

"I want to do it. My family's counting on me."

"Just be careful," Rebecca says.

Nick climbs slowly, sweat gathering at his brow despite the cool air. The dust is thicker up here, untouched for years. He reaches the panel and wipes a small circle clean with his sleeve, revealing a single keyhole.

"Of course it needs a damn key," he mutters. "Anyone seen one of those lying around?"

"I've got a gun," Parmen offers, raising his eyebrows.

"No!" Tericia and Lester say in unison.

"We can't risk damaging the controls," Tericia adds.

"There's a tiny lip on one side," Nick calls. "I might be able to pry it open, if we find something thin enough."

"Climb down. Let's look for tools," Tericia instructs.

Everyone fans out again. Tericia heads toward the old workshop. Lester searches the medical bay and tool closets. Rebecca, surprisingly nimble despite the stress of the day, joins her kids rummaging through drawers of obsolete maintenance kits.

Parmen stays behind, leaning on the stair railing, watching the panel above.

A few minutes pass.

Then a single, sharp sound pierces the air.

CRACK!

The gunshot reverberates down the corridors.

"Parmen!" Lester yells, sprinting back toward the stairwell.

Nick and Tericia aren't far behind.

"What the fuck, Parmen!?" Lester barks, skidding to a stop.

"Yeah, asshole!" Nick echoes, shoving him against the wall.

"Hey!" Tericia shouts, raising her voice. "Everyone shut up!"

The silence that follows is broken only by the fading ring of the gunshot in their ears.

Parmen, leaning heavily against the wall, wipes sweat from his brow. "I was hungry. Didn't want to wait another twelve hours to maybe eat stale protein bars."

"You're un-fucking-believable," Nick says, shaking his head.

"I'm effective," Parmen replies. "Look up."

Nick climbs again. When his head clears the top of the ladder, he gasps.

The panel is open.

Inside are three analog switch sets labeled Door 1, Door 2, and Door 3. Each has toggles marked OPEN, CLOSE, and STOP.

"Somehow you didn't hit anything important," Nick mutters, partially impressed, partially annoyed.

"Told you it was just as good as a key," Parmen says with a grin.

"Pick one," Tericia says. "Doesn't matter. My guess is they all lead to the same access corridor."

Nick presses the OPEN switch for Door 2. The closest level to where everyone is standing.

A deep groan rumbles through the building—metal resisting the command. Decades of rust grind against ancient gears. The noise is loud, scraping, unsettling.

"Stop it there," Tericia says once it opens enough for them to pass. Nick toggles STOP.

The team ascends to the corridor, stepping through the half-open door. Beyond it lies a ramp, wide enough for supply carts or emergency vehicles. It snakes upward into dim light.

Tericia smiles. "I knew it. Three doors for redundancy. And likely access to each level for evacuation or delivery purposes."

The group continues cautiously up the ramp. They see how the ramp splits to the three levels, showing each one reaching a corresponding panel that they found was different. The smell of aged metal and stale air gives way to something new—fresh air. Even the kids feel it.

Then Tericia halts. "We need someone to stay and watch this place. Lester, I think you should stay."

Lester stops short. "Seriously?"

"You're probably plastered across every news feed on Earth. Tems made sure of it. If you're seen out there, it could end badly for all of us," Tericia says to Lester.

"She's right," Nick adds quietly. "You'd put us all at risk."

Lester's jaw clenches, but he nods. "Fine. I'll stay. I'm not thrilled about it, but I get it."

"Parmen, you also stay and get in that fucking bed, let the medical gear fix you up," Tericia continues.

"I'm good," Parmen says in a nonchalant tone.

"Bullshit. You heal or you are no good to this group," Tericia declares.

"Fine," Parmen says with a huff.

"Lester, guard the bunker. Keep Holepunch safe. Keep Parmen in that bed. And if we don't return soon—"

"Don't say it," Lester cuts her off. "Just hurry back."

"We'll bring food, fuel, and hopefully a little good news," Tericia says, her tone both confident and weary, then over to playful. "Anything else you need from the store, honey?"

"Funny," Lester says dryly, watching them go.

As the group disappears up the ramp, he turns and looks back at the dim corridors behind him. Trapped, but for a completely different reason than before.

CHAPTER 26

Nick and Tericia crest the top of the concrete ramp after a mile long walk, the cool breath of aged earth still clinging to their clothes. Behind them, Nick's wife and daughters cling tightly to one another, hovering far closer than necessary. Tericia, though she doesn't say it out loud, finds their proximity claustrophobic. Every step feels like wading through invisible tension. But she knows better than to push them away—trauma isn't something easily shaken, and being close is their defense.

"Are you sure you're okay with them coming with us?" Nick asks, glancing sideways. His voice is hushed, as though afraid the presence of his family might break something delicate.

Tericia had convinced Nick and his family that they would easily be hunted down by Borvil if they went out on their own. They would be just as stuck as the rest of the group until Borvil is no longer able to attack.

"Of course," Tericia replies, pausing for a moment and glancing back at the girls. "Whoever might be looking for us… they won't expect this. They'll be hunting for fugitives, for fugitives with weapons and edge—not for a tired-looking man with a wife, two daughters, and an aunt. A family unit screams harmless. We're less likely to draw attention, and right now, that's the only kind of power we have."

She lowers herself to a squat in front of Nick's girls. Her expression softens, eyes locking with theirs. "But for that to work," she says gently, "you two need to smile. No more sad faces, okay? Sad faces make people worry. Happy faces? Happy faces make us invisible."

The girls glance nervously at their parents. Nick nods encouragingly, Rebecca offering a small but warm smile that soon becomes contagious. Slowly, like sunlight breaking through cloud cover, the girls' faces brighten.

Tericia smiles back, then rises, brushing the dust from her knees. "That's more like it."

She leads them forward to the sealed blast hatch at the top of the slope. The massive circular door is dark with age and grime, framed by thick metal and concrete. Rust trails down like veins across its surface, and the locking lever is stiff and motionless.

"I don't know what's on the other side," she says, eyeing the mechanism. "Could be a collapsed hill, a flooded chamber, or a clean path to sunlight. But we've got a destination. I know roughly where we are. That's all we can ask for at the moment."

"We do?" Nick asks, blinking.

"Oh. Right," Tericia mutters, snapping her fingers. "I'm the only one who knows where we are."

Nick cocks a brow.

"We're in rural Virginia," she reveals.

Nick whistles low. "You think we can make it to DC? The fuel depot there is our best shot, but with 'traitor' floating around like a wanted poster in every database, it won't exactly be a tourist walk."

"I don't think we'll have to make it all the way to DC or any large labs," Tericia replies, stepping forward. "I have an idea."

She grips the lever and pulls. Nothing. The handle may as well have been welded shut. She plants her feet, yanks again, and again—still nothing. Her arms tremble with effort.

"Glad I brought the sledgehammer," Nick says with a tired grin, passing his family a gentle wave to stay back. He hefts the weight of it over his shoulder and swings down. The first impact rings out like a thunderclap in the enclosed corridor. Dust rains from the seams. He swings again. And again.

"Come on, you stubborn bastard," Nick mutters, sweat pouring from his brow.

After several strikes, a groan escapes the latch. Just a twitch of movement. He lets the hammer fall, his breath ragged.

Tericia steps up, catching the handle as Nick stumbles back. Without missing a beat, she lifts the sledgehammer high and slams it down. On the second hit, the latch clanks fully open, released from its eternal seal. With a hiss of equalizing air pressure, the massive hatch cracks open.

"Loosened it for you," Nick wheezes, slumping against the wall.

With a grin, Tericia puts the hammer aside and pulls the door wider. A low groan echoes from the hinges, and stale, ancient air exhales from the chamber. The tunnel beyond is pure shadow, the only light coming from the glow of their flashlights as they squeeze through.

The tunnel ends abruptly in a curved wall, blocking their exit. But to the right, Tericia spots a narrow recess, only a meter deep. In its center is a small, nearly invisible latch.

"Gotcha," she murmurs, gripping the lever and pulling it open. A second wave of air rushes past as sunlight pierces the darkness. Everyone squints into the sudden brilliance. The contrast is so severe it momentarily blinds them.

One by one, they climb through and find themselves in an old mausoleum. The air smells faintly of stone, dust, and dried flowers. The marble walls are lined with burial slots, each marked with names and dates. But two stand out— generic names carved without flourish.

Thomas Johnson. Jessica Smith.

No photos. No epitaphs. Just stone markers. Tericia runs her fingers over the surface and smiles.

"No one would question this. Two of the most common names you could pick. Untraceable. No significance. Just a lie that hides the truth," she says, mostly to herself.

Nick and his family climb out behind her. The girls peer around curiously while Tericia inspects the latch on both sides of the markers. Nothing obvious to reopen it once outside.

"We can't leave it unsecured," she mutters. "We can't risk anyone stumbling on it."

"There's no outside latch. I don't think it was ever meant to open from out here," Nick observes.

Tericia gives him a sarcastic thumbs-up. "Thanks for that, Captain Obvious."

She looks around for anything she can use. Her eyes land on the girls playing with old skeins of decorative yarn left in a dusty urn.

"Mind if I borrow that?" she asks.

They hand it over without a word. Tericia returns to the tunnel and threads the yarn over the latch in a simple pulley loop. After several tries, she works out a tension system that will let them re-latch the door from the outside. It's clumsy but effective.

Finally, she arranges the yarn into loose braids, laying it across the stone faces of the mausoleum niches, trying to make it blend in like part of the memorial decor.

"It's not perfect, but it'll hold until we're back," she says.

"I just hope no one finds it and wonders why someone gave Jessica Smith a loom tribute," Nick replies dryly.

They chuckle together, stepping out of the mausoleum into open air.

Outside, sunlight pours down through a thin veil of clouds. Grass sways gently in the wind. They are in a graveyard, aged and overgrown, headstones scattered and cracked. The hills roll outward into trees, and in the far distance, a transitway can just barely be seen winding toward civilization.

The silence hangs between them. There's no sign of surveillance, no drones, no black vans parked nearby. Just the whisper of wind and the weight of their next steps.

CHAPTER 27

Tericia, Nick, and his family stand at the rusted cemetery gate, peering through the iron bars like ghosts of a forgotten time, watching the modern world stream past them. Ground vehicles hum and whir down the old road, some gliding on wheels, others levitating slightly above the surface. Overhead, a stream of airborne traffic slices across the sky—flying taxis, courier drones, and personal skimmers dart past like metallic birds. Sleek single-rider pods zip by on magnetic lanes with uncanny precision.

Nick adjusts his stance, shielding his family instinctively. "We need a taxi," he mutters. "We can't stand here long. Someone's going to notice us."

Tericia gives a short shake of her head. "No taxis. They're all monitored. Video records get uploaded instantly to traffic enforcement and security databases. The moment one of us steps inside, we're flagged, tracked, and boxed in."

Nick's mouth tightens into a hard line. "So we just stand here and wait to be noticed anyway? We look like fugitives already."

"Technically, we are," Tericia replies, her tone calm, but resolute. "What we need are three pop speeders. Small. Fast. Easy to maneuver. And with your girls riding pillion, we'll blend into the city like a family on a joyride."

Nick looks at her, incredulous. "You're serious? You want to steal them?"

"Borrow indefinitely," she says with a shrug. "Nobody's going to give them to us willingly."

"You want to make my wife and kids complicit in grand theft auto?"

"I want them alive," Tericia answers, her tone sharpening. "Borvil doesn't take hostages. They eliminate witnesses. We play this straight and slow, we die. That's not an exaggeration, Nick. You've seen what they're capable of."

Nick glances at Rebecca. She's holding their daughters close, their small faces tense with confusion and fear. He sighs and nods. "Fine. Let's get it over with."

The group steps past the wrought-iron gate and onto the edge of the high-speed single-rider lane. Tericia waits, eyes scanning for the right opportunity. A pop speeder—a compact, mono-wheel vehicle with a seat hovering just high enough for a person to sit—buzzes toward them. She steps forward, waving both arms.

The rider slows down, confused, then pulls off to the shoulder. He dismounts, eyebrows raised, scanning the group. "You look... familiar," he says slowly, eyes narrowing on Tericia. "I know you from somewhere, but I can't quite—"

"Thanks for stopping," Tericia says sweetly, moving behind the gate and motioning for the guy to follow. Once behind the gate and out of view, she makes her demand. "We need your speeder."

The man's face goes blank. "Wait, what?"

"And your device chip," she adds, drawing her weapon.

The man recoils, lifting his hands in disbelief. "Whoa—what the hell? You can't be serious."

"I was polite," Tericia replies. "But we're on borrowed time."

"I can't give you the chip! It's embedded!"

Tericia tilts her head. "We can remove it."

Before the man can react, Tericia steps forward and knocks him out cold with the butt of her gun. He crumples to the ground. Nick flinches.

"Get the chip," Tericia orders, already peering past the gate, scanning the road for their next mark.

"Are you serious?" Nick asks, his voice low. "I'm not cutting into someone's wrist."

Tericia turns, her voice softer. "It's embedded in the dorsal wrist, just under the skin. He won't even feel it—he's unconscious. We've got a window, now use your knife."

"How are you so calm about this? How do you do this with great ease?" Nick asks, making sure he is between Tericia and his family. "You're starting to frighten me. Starting to act too much like Tems."

"Ten years of torture, watching others do these things, being a scientist and understanding what works and what doesn't. All of that will change a person," Tericia responds, then steps toward Nick. She places a hand on his shoulder in a reassuring fashion, "I'm not happy about this either, but our survival demands such actions. Once Borvil has been put in its place and real legislation has been put in place surrounding wormhole technology, will I truly feel at ease and can go back to just being a scientist."

Nick nods in understanding.

"And don't ever... EVER... compare me to that monster," Tericia says firmly, looking directly into Nick's eyes.

Nick nods again, looks at his knife, then looks at the guy.

"Hurry, before I flag someone else down," Tericia commands.

Nick hesitates, then glances at his daughters. One of them watches with wide, silent eyes. The other buries her face in her mother's coat. With a grimace, Nick kneels by the unconscious man and proceeds to remove the chip.

Two more pop speeders follow the same script. Tericia waves them down, feigning distress, and when they stop, she disables them with swift, efficient strikes. Nick extracts the chips, hands trembling with each incision. Blood stains his sleeves. His hands shake as he wipes them on the grass.

When it's over, three bodies lie lined up beside the old cemetery wall, wrists cut open, vehicle chips removed and clutched in Nick's reddened hands.

"What do we do with them?" he asks, voice low, almost hollow.

Tericia pulls out a small scanning pad and snaps images of each man's face. "I logged their biometric markers. If we survive this, I'll find them. We'll make it right."

Nick stares at her, jaw clenched. "If we survive."

Tericia kneels beside his daughters, her expression softening. "I'm sorry you had to see that," she says gently. "This isn't the way things should be. But bad people are in charge right now. We're going to change that, and unfortunately, we have to be bad to catch up to them."

The girls don't speak. One offers a cautious nod. The other silently clings to her mother's leg.

Nick hands out the chips, one to Tericia, one to his wife, and one in his pocket. He then lifts his daughter into his lap with him as he gets on his speeder. His wife does the same with the second, and Tericia climbs aboard the third.

"Where to?" Nick asks, glancing back over his shoulder realizing that the speeders hold steady without falling over.

"Louisville," Tericia says over the breeze. "We're headed to a place near Fort Knox."

Nick arches an eyebrow. "That's... not subtle. Lots of surveillance around there."

"No. Not subtle. There's a military-grade Xomithrine facility near there. Off the map. Unmarked. I helped build it."

"You're kidding."

"I never kid about quantum fuel reserves," Tericia replies, grinning. "Follow my lead. Stay close. We move fast and stay off the main routes. These speeders aren't tracked unless they get reported. We've got a few hours at best."

Nick nods and leans forward. The pop speeder hums to life and juts forward. The gyroscopic balance system kicks in, stabilizing under the weight. Tericia shifts forward and takes the lead.

They shoot forward in a blur, leaving behind the graves, the blood, and the quiet ghosts of a dying world. Tericia rides in silence, her hair streaming behind her, mind fixed on the path ahead.

Nick stays close, eyes bouncing between the road and his girls clinging tightly behind him. Beside him, Rebecca leans low on her own speeder, her jaw set in a grim line of determination.

The sun begins to dip low on the horizon, casting long shadows across the trees lining the old roads. As they ride, the sound of wind replaces the noise of fear, if only for a little while.

In that brief moment—between the cemetery and whatever came next—they are no longer fugitives.

They are a family on the move.

A mission in motion.

A threat to the empire that stole everything from them.

CHAPTER 28

Tericia moves like a shadow possessed, her mind driven by fury, focus, and urgency. She leans forward with purposeful, relentless. She barrels forward through the winding trails of rural Virginia like a predator tracking its prey. Nick struggles to match her pace, the extra weight of his daughter, slowing him down. Rebecca, with their other daughter, further behind also having trouble catching up.

Every few miles, Tericia slows. She doesn't say anything. She simply waits, staring at them with a mix of annoyance and resignation as they finally go past, only to have Tericia take the lead again, shortly after, planning the next leg of their journey.

They stop at the edge of the Kentucky state line, hiding just behind a road sign off the side of an old road.

"This is the line," Tericia says, keeping her voice low. "Once we cross, we'll be seen. Cameras, surveillance satellites, drones, the whole fucking array. They'll know we're here. Which means every second we waste is one closer to being caught."

Rebecca leans forward, her shoulders tense. "Are you sure bringing the kids is the right choice? Maybe we should hide them—"

"Don't," Tericia interrupts, slicing through Rebecca's concern with a razor-sharp tone. "We have to stick together. It is the only way that they might not give us a second look."

Rebecca starts to speak, maybe to argue, but one look at Tericia's eyes—dark with exhaustion and filled with something dangerously close to grief—and she backs down. Her nod is small. Defeated.

"Good," Tericia mutters, more to herself than anyone else. She glances at the children and adds, a bit softer, "They'll be okay. But we have to move fast."

They mount the pop speeders and cross the state line.

Immediately, they're under the eyes of the network. Cameras mounted on overpasses rotate. Drones buzz in the distance. The roads have eyes, and those eyes are hungry.

Tericia darts through side roads, zipping around forgotten county lanes and into stretches of rural emptiness. The others trail behind like fragile comets trying to chase a collapsing star. They race past old towns, empty strip malls, and other remains from a bygone era that chose not to progress like larger cities. The further they get from the state line, the more the fear of capture closes in.

Eventually, Tericia veers off onto a narrow gravel path near Shepherdsville. It's a small town that has little to offer. She stops near an unmarked shoulder just wide enough for the speeders to idle. She dismounts, eyes scanning the road behind them.

Nick rolls to a stop beside her, panting. "What is it? What's wrong?"

"We should've been chased," Tericia says without looking at him. Her voice is low, tense.

"What?" Rebecca asks, dismounting and lifting her daughter off the speeder.

"There was no pursuit," Tericia says. "No drones. No intercept squads. No digital ghosts. That's not right."

"You were expecting one?" Nick asks, confused and suddenly more nervous.

"Always," Tericia replies. "I planned for it. Improvised tactics. Emergency protocols. But the fact that we weren't followed… that means one of two things. Either they're incompetent…" she trails off.

"Or?" Rebecca presses.

"Or they're waiting for us."

The silence that follows hits like a gunshot.

Still, Tericia turns to the woods. "We're here now. No turning back. We need fuel or we die."

They hike into the dense undergrowth. A trail barely visible through the brush winds its way toward a shadowy grove. Tericia leads them with the confidence of someone following an internal map. A quarter mile later, they see a large cave entrance, and without pause, Tericia walks inside. The follow the paths of heavy equipment until those tracks veer off into a wall. They stand before a wide, moss-covered rock wall. Tericia steps forward, scanning the surface. She finds it—a stone slightly protruding. She presses it.

The wall groans.

A hidden passage opens, revealing a corridor cut from concrete and steel, glowing softly with embedded lights.

The moment they step in, the outer door slides shut behind them.

Nick glances over his shoulder. "We're really doing this."

Tericia nods. "Welcome to a hidden military supply cache. Most supplies needed by the military are found here. They don't have guards because posting guards would give it away. Fort Knox, being so close, keeps people interested and they don't look nearby."

They follow the hallway until it opens into a massive underground cargo bay. Racks line the walls, filled with sealed crates. Tericia moves forward cautiously, then halts mid-step.

The lights die.

The air shifts.

The children scream.

Footsteps echo. Voices. Weapons being raised. Shadows shift and multiply.

Tericia whispers, "Shit."

The lights flicker back on—harsh, blinding. Dozens of armed guards encircle them. And stepping out from behind their line is the ghost she most hoped to never see again.

Tems.

He's smiling. He's alive. His right arm and leg aren't missing as Tericia expected. Instead, they look different. Not human.

"I've got to hand it to you," he says, walking slowly into the center. "When Lester closed the wormhole and my arm and leg were departed from my body, I thought I was a goner. But being rich has its rewards. The best care and really fast service. The newest tech…" he says the last part, holding up his right hand, admiring it.

"You definitely threw me off. I was expecting you would end up in DC. To the science institute. Your old home," Tems continues.

She stays still, eyes blazing. "I expected you'd wait for us there. Figured this might be the path you ignored."

"Well," he shrugs, "I was in DC. But then you showed up in Kentucky. Surveillance gave you away. I knew this was your play as soon as you popped up on my radar. You're good. But not that good. And pop speeders are slow compared to what I have."

He then turns and scans the group. His eyes settle on Rebecca, then the children.

"No," Tericia snaps, stepping forward. "They're not involved—"

Tems silences her with a wave and a smirk. He moves to Rebecca and strokes her cheek like a man inspecting a possession. Then he crouches and places his hand atop the girls' heads.

They flinch. One of them sobs.

Nick lunges forward.

Guards descend instantly, dragging him back. Rebecca cries out, pulling her children close. The guards grip her arms. She resists. It doesn't matter.

"Stop it!" Tericia yells. "Leave them alone!"

Tems steps toward her slowly, measured like a predator circling its prize.

"Now, you're in no position to demand anything," he says, raising his voice just enough to echo through the chamber.

Nick is hauled backward. Rebecca, too. The girls scream now, calling for their father, for their mother. The sound burns through Tericia's ears like acid.

Guards drag the entire family out of view, Nick looking back, desperate for Tericia to do something until they can no longer maintain eye contact.

Then it's quiet again.

Tems turns to Tericia. "What should I do with you?" he asks, but before she can answer—

"Don't! Speak!"

His voice explodes across the room. He closes the gap between them and grabs her by the face with his new hand, forcing her chin up, squeezing with violent force, harder than any human could.

"I should put a bullet between your eyes right here," he hisses. "But then I'd never get the device. I might have been in your bunker, but we never did get its location."

"It's useless," Tericia spits through her unmovable jaw. "Out of fuel."

"I know that, you idiot," Tems snaps. "Why do you think I'm here? You think I want a reunion? I want that device working again. And you're going to help me. Right up until I don't need you anymore."

Tericia's lip curls. "Go to hell."

Tems backhands her. The blow knocks her sideways. She stumbles and falls to the floor, catching herself on her elbow with a yelp of pain.

Tems points his gun at her head. "Get her to the medical room," he barks at his guards. "Before I change my mind and redecorate this floor with her brains."

Two guards lift Tericia roughly to her feet.

Tems leans in one last time, his breath hot on her neck. "If I don't get what I want, I'll show you what it's like in hell."

He smiles.

She doesn't scream. Doesn't cry.

She just stares ahead. And in the pit of her stomach, she knows this isn't over.

It's just beginning.

CHAPTER 29

"There's no use struggling, Tericia," Tems says, his voice slithering through the air like oil. He stands a few paces away, his silhouette lit by the cold overhead lights. In his hand, he holds a gleaming pair of surgical pliers, their tips perfect, unused, and every glint of a light a reminder of the depth of Tems's resources. "You're going to tell me where the device is, or you won't. If you do, things get a little easier for you. If not… well…"

He snaps the pliers together, the metallic click echoing through the sterile room. Each snap is deliberate, rhythmic. A countdown. A threat.

"I'd rather die than let you have unlimited access to the universe, you corrupt piece of shit," Tericia spits, her voice raw, the last syllables sharp as broken glass.

Tems tilts his head, amused. "You always were dramatic," he says, crouching by her feet. "But let's not be hasty. There's still so much of you left to break."

He presses the pliers against her pinky toe, steady and slow, adjusting his grip like an artist preparing for a delicate stroke, making sure he only has the toenail gripped. Tericia flinches, sucking in a sharp breath through gritted teeth, trying to brace for what's coming. Her fists clench against the restraints, nails biting into her palms.

Tems pulls.

A scream tears through her. She's not sure if it comes from her mouth or her mind. The pain is hot, immediate, and radiates all the way to her skull.

Then he stops.

Tems lets go of the nail—still attached, and bleeding—and straightens with a smug smile. "You see, if I actually finish pulling them off, there's a limit to what I can do. That's what I got wrong last time. But this?" He taps the tender, hanging nail with the pliers. "This gives us so much more time together. So much for you to enjoy. So much for me to savor."

He moves to the next toe.

Tericia doesn't scream this time, not immediately. She grinds her jaw, forces her body to remain still. She will not give him the satisfaction again. But when the pliers tighten, and he pulls without warning, the pain again surges past her threshold and a guttural cry escapes her lips.

Her vision blurs. Her chest heaves. But her stare never leaves him.

"Where is Nick and his family?" she gasps, trying to think about something else—anything else.

Tems casually wipes a drop of sweat from his brow. "Oh, they're safe. For now."

He looks down at her, his face darkening. "Have you ever seen what a parent does when their child is threatened?"

Tericia's breath catches.

Tems leans in, his face inches from hers. His breath smells like mint and cruelty. "Anything. That's what they'll do.

Anything." He stands again, walking a slow circle around her. "Nick already gave us everything. Where you've been. Where you were headed. What you think of me. He just needed a little... encouragement."

"You're lying," Tericia hisses, though her voice lacks conviction. "You've been here with me this whole time. You don't know that."

Tems stops behind her and leans close to her ear. "He cried. Said he was sorry. But in the end? He cracked." He then makes sure Tericia can see him as he turns his head and shows his earpiece, the only thing he needs to show her to prove what he knows.

He moves back to her feet and resumes his work, tugging each toenail just enough to cause agony but not release. Tericia tries to scream, but her throat is ragged now. The pain blooms in every nerve ending, her brain struggling to keep up, to stay conscious, to think.

She begins to count silently. Prime numbers. A technique to remain grounded. 2. 3. 5. 7. 11. 13...

"It's been too long," Lester mutters, pacing the dim corridor like a caged animal. His arms are folded tightly, knuckles white, voice tight with worry.

Parmen leans back against the wall, wincing as he shifts to find a position that doesn't make him flinch. "Yeah," he agrees. "Too long." A beat of silence. "But what can we do, Lester? We don't even know where they went. Hell, we don't even know if they made it."

"She's brilliant," Lester says, more to himself than anyone else. "But sometimes brilliance becomes a kind of blindness. She thinks fast, but she doesn't always stop to consider all the options."

"You think she made the wrong move?"

"I think she went straight for the Xomithrine instead of the components to make it ourselves," Lester says, finally stopping to lean on a crate. "It's exactly what I would've done. Which is why Tems probably expected it too."

Parmen grunts, shifting his weight. "So, where would she go? If you had to guess?"

"DC," Lester answers without hesitation. "Biggest government lab still functioning. Last I knew, they had the largest Xomithrine production capacity on the East Coast. Or to her old scientific stomping grounds, also in DC. Either way, the answer is DC."

Parmen raises a brow. "That's assuming we're even on the East Coast."

"Right," Lester groans, frustrated. "There are dozens of labs scattered across the U.S., but we don't even know what state we're in. That's the problem."

"Then I guess," Parmen says slowly, dragging out the words like he's trying to make them settle deeper, "we go outside and find out where we are. Step one. Simple recon."

"And then what?" Lester asks. "Hope she's fine? March into a guarded facility and try to rescue her? If she's already been taken—"

"Suicide," Parmen finishes for him. "If she's caught, you wouldn't survive two minutes getting close. No, you want to help her?" He shifts, breathing through the pain. "Then you build a way to help her."

Lester stares.

"You find the components. The materials. You make your own Xomithrine. You fire up the device," Parmen says. "And then, you hunt down the bastard who took her. You find her if she hasn't been captured. Whatever."

Lester's eyes sharpen with realization. "That sounds like the best idea yet. Become self-sufficient. Then find someone at Borvil to tell me where she is."

"Now you're thinking like a soldier," Parmen says, a faint grin curling the side of his mouth.

Lester exhales slowly, a shaky smile spreading across his face. "You know... you're kind of terrifying when you're right."

Parmen waves him off. "Go. I'll watch the device. And keep recovering, apparently. You make the next move."

Lester nods, turns, then pauses. "Be ready for anything."

"Always."

Lester ascends the ramp two steps at a time, emerging into the mausoleum. The air is stale, but cool. He finds the yarn Tericia used to mask the exit and carefully adjusts it to make the seams of the hatch vanish into the stone façade. It's not perfect, but close enough to avoid suspicion.

He steps out into the daylight and squints at the sky. The world feels... too normal. Vehicles of different types hum in the distance, birds chirp in the trees, and the wind rustles leaves with an indifference that stings.

He walks toward the main cemetery path, keeping his head down, trying to blend into the backdrop. If his face is scanned, if any recognition software catches even a glimpse, he could be arrested within minutes.

He stops at the exit gate, watching traffic crawl by. "Can't risk a taxi," he mutters to himself. "Every cab logs passengers. Photos, timestamps, GPS... They'd find me before I left the block."

So he waits.

Minutes drag by. Then, finally, a nondescript ground vehicle turns into the cemetery. Black, boxy, with no markings. Funeral transport, maybe. The kind no one questions. It moves toward a low structure that looks like a crematorium.

Lester starts walking after it, keeping his distance, his eyes on the gravel path. Just a mourner taking a stroll. Nothing to see here.

As the vehicle stops and the driver exits, Lester quickens his pace and slides in through the passenger door. The cabin smells faintly of pine and hot coffee. His pulse hammers in his ears.

"I've never stolen a vehicle before," he whispers, his fingers trembling as they hover near the dashboard. "Not even sure where to start."

He looks around helplessly. No keyed ignition, just a button. Some modern panel flickers quietly with a waiting prompt. He swallows hard and sinks lower into the seat, clutching the small pistol Parmen gave him days ago.

He hears footsteps returning. His stomach drops.

The driver—middle-aged, balding, wearing a wrinkled uniform—opens the door and climbs in. Before he even looks forward, he's laughing and calling out a final goodbye to someone inside. Then he turns... and freezes.

"Best not to scream," Lester says, gun now steady in his hand.

The man blinks at him. "Whoa. Okay. Sure."

"Start the car. Just drive. Anywhere."

The man studies Lester for a moment. "You're not a pro. I can tell. You're sweating like a faucet."

"Still holding a gun," Lester warns.

"Noted," the man replies. "Name's Dave, by the way. In case you decide not to shoot me."

Lester blinks. "Dave?"

"Yep. Been driving this sucker for twenty years. Seen some weird stuff. Never thought I'd end up in a hostage situation, but hey—first time for everything."

"I'm not holding you hostage. I need help."

Dave shrugs. "Okay. Where to?"

Lester hesitates. "I need supplies. Materials. Lab-grade. Exotic metals, stabilized compounds, maybe even a centrifuge."

Dave lets out a low whistle. "You planning to build a bomb?"

"No. A wormhole."

Dave tilts his head. "Like... the sci-fi kind? You're serious?"

Lester gives him a look that says you don't know the half of it.

Dave squints at him. "You one of them? From that group they're calling traitors?"

Lester doesn't answer.

"Well, I'm in," Dave says with a grin. "Been living a boring-ass life since 2043. One thing I have always wanted to do was be a getaway driver. What's your name?"

"Les..." Lester pauses before finishing, realizing he doesn't want to give his real name. "Lesley," he finishes.

They shake hands.

"Lesley it is. Tell me what the job is," Dave replies.

"How would you like to visit another planet?" Lester asks with a smile.

"If there's a chance I can go to another planet before I die, I'm definitely your driver. You don't even have to ask twice."

Lester lowers the gun slowly. "You're insane."

"I prefer underchallenged. And don't worry—my silence comes cheap."

"Alright, Dave." Lester exhales for the first time in what feels like days. "Where are we know?"

"You don't know?" Dave asks.

"Nope. Didn't come here by normal means," Lester replies.

"That's a cryptic statement. We are in Virginia. Wherever we are headed, you're going to have to explain a lot of things," Dave says with a giddy smile, like a man who is finally getting to live out a dream.

"Oh. It's a long story. Head for Charlotte," Lester says, finally having a sense of ease about Dave.

Dave hits the ignition. "Charlotte it is. Hope you're good at making lists, cause I'm gonna need to know every single thing you want to steal."

Lester lets his head fall back against the seat and closes his eyes for a moment.

'*We're coming, Tericia. Just hang on.*'

"And then I tried to steal your truck," Lester says with a rueful half-smile, glancing over at Dave as the truck approaches the state line into North Carolina.

Dave snorts. "That's a lot to take in." He shakes his head, a grin tugging at the corner of his mouth. "Still wrapping my head around that part of your story, by the way. You found another planet—with buildings on it."

Lester nods. "That's where I want to go when this is all over. Back to that planet. Back to science."

Dave whistles. "Well, for now, you've gotta survive. If even half of what you told me about Borvil and that Tems guy is true, crossing this state line's about to get real dicey."

"I'll manage," Lester mutters.

"No," Dave counters. "You'll hide. The seat you're sitting on—it lifts. There's a hidden compartment underneath. Use it for smuggling contraband back and forth. Sometimes I take an extra job as I am rolling through. Companies don't like it. And they don't need to know. You might fit."

Lester raises an eyebrow. "'Might'?"

Dave shrugs. "Don't know how flexible you are, mister Lesley man."

Grumbling, Lester shifts off the seat. Dave pops it open. The hidden cavity is dark and just barely big enough for someone to contort into. Lester climbs in and curls into the fetal position, limbs pressed tight against the cramped metal walls.

"Drive fast or I'm going to suffocate," he warns as Dave closes the compartment lid with a chuckle. "And my name isn't Lesley, if you hadn't caught on."

"I know," Dave replies with a wink.

As the truck rolls across the state line, Dave tries to stay relaxed behind the wheel, but the dozens of surveillance towers peppered along the route keep pulling his attention. A thin sheen of sweat builds along his brow. He wipes it away, eyes darting from each side mirror to the road.

A few minutes later, he pulls into a rest stop, heart thudding in his chest. "Hang tight," he says to the compartment. "Just a little longer."

"Hurry!" Lester's voice is muffled, strained. "I'm in pain!"

"You'll be in more pain if you come out early," Dave says gently. "Just breathe slow."

Then: a knock.

Dave freezes. The knock comes again, harder this time. He forces his expression into something nonchalant and swings the driver's door open.

A soldier with an assault rifle stares back. His face is tense, jaw locked.

"Did you find him?"

"Find who?" Dave asks, injecting just enough confusion into his tone to sound genuine.

"Don't play dumb. You were supposed to go to that cemetery. You were told to find someone named Lester. And now you are here. So, either you found him or you left your post."

Dave's pulse spikes, but his face stays neutral. "Nobody was there. Just some guy in the crematorium. We laughed about his name being Dave too. Bit of a coincidence. Besides, I got called down here for a pickup. Didn't abandon anything, just reassigned."

The soldier scowls. "Open the back of the truck!"

Dave sighs theatrically. "Of course. Wouldn't want to slow down your very important witch hunt."

He gets out slowly and heads to the rear of the truck. Meanwhile, the soldier climbs into the cab, inspecting every surface. Lester, hidden just below him, holds his breath, fighting the burn in his lungs. He feels his heartbeat thundering in his ears.

"It's open!" Dave calls out.

The soldier emerges from the cab and heads to the back, where he clambers in and starts banging on panels, checking seams, kicking bolts. He's thorough, and looking for a hidden compartment. A newly stripped screw, perhaps. Something revealing deception.

"Can you hurry this along?" Dave says. "I have a pickup in an hour."

The soldier freezes. "Trying to rush me, huh?" He jumps down and levels the rifle at Dave's chest. "What are you hiding?"

"Nothing! Just—time is money, alright? If I'm late, I lose the job. I don't even know this Lester guy! I go where I am told and pick up what I am supposed to pick up. Sorry that your guy wasn't there."

The two men lock eyes. The tension stretches.

Finally, the soldier lowers his weapon and spits on the ground. "Tems is gonna be pissed."

Dave blinks. "Tems?"

"The guy who hired you, dipshit."

"Oh," Dave mutters. "Didn't get a name. Just a pickup location and time. That's how it usually goes for me."

The soldier grunts and walks off without another word. He gets in his car and peels out.

Once he's out of sight, Dave climbs back into the cab and starts the truck. "Safe to come out," he calls as they merge back onto the highway.

The seat lifts with a hiss of compressed air, and Lester unfolds himself slowly, groaning as his joints pop.

"I am definitely too old for this," he mumbles, massaging his arms and legs. "I think I just shaved a year off my life."

Dave chuckles. "Well, you're still breathing. That's a win."

Lester eyes him with suspicion. "You knew I was at the cemetery. You were sent to find me. So why didn't you turn me in?"

Dave shrugs, keeping his eyes on the road. "I think they just sent guys like me to every cemetery in the area. Dispatch wouldn't give specifics but there were definitely a lot of strange orders today. And I didn't turn you in because I decided I liked your story better than Tems's paycheck."

Lester frowns. "That doesn't make sense. You could have been killed for...wait. What!? Did you say Tems."

"No. The soldier dude said Tems. I just used his name because I don't know who is actually going to sign that paycheck," Dave replies. "You said you killed him, yes?"

"Okay. Yes, Tems should be dead. Maybe that soldier doesn't know yet," Lester says, contemplation hiding behind his eyes.

Dave finally looks over. "Anyway, you're a scientist who discovered another planet. That's the kind of story that doesn't come along every day. I want in. Not just some paycheck turning over some guy."

Lester studies him. "You're serious."

"Dead serious. I want to go to that planet with you. Become the first interstellar delivery driver or whatever."

A brief smile pulls at Lester's lips, but it doesn't last. "Borvil knows about cemeteries. That shouldn't be possible unless..."

He stops, the implication hitting him like a brick.

"Unless someone spoke. Gave up the goods. Squealed," Dave finishes.

Lester nods, giving Dave a disapproving side glance, then looking back toward the road, face grim. "Nick wouldn't betray us...unless Borvil had his family. That company would absolutely use them against him."

He sits back, gears turning in his mind. "We need to move fast. Faster than I thought. Borvil already has too much of a head start."

Dave grips the steering wheel tighter. "We'll move fast— but I'm not stupid. I've seen what happens to people who speed around here. They get stopped and questioned. Going slow is the fastest way forward."

Lester stares out the window, his fists clenched. "Tericia's out there. If Borvil has her, I don't care how crazy the plan is. I'm going to get her back."

Dave doesn't say anything at first. But after a long silence, he nods.

"Then let's get you what you need to do it."

The truck speeds into the horizon, a man with a broken past and a delivery driver living out his fantasies, chasing hope on a road paved with danger.

CHAPTER 31

Dave grips the steering wheel tighter than necessary, his knuckles pale against the cracked vinyl. The hum of tires on worn asphalt fills the silence between him and Lester, who sits stiffly in the passenger seat, hunched forward like he's preparing for a crash that hasn't come yet.

Charlotte looms ahead, a jagged silhouette of metal and glass. The city's neon arteries pulse faintly against the deepening dusk, and the distant buzz of air traffic only adds to the anxiety slowly building in Lester's gut.

"Pull in like you're making a delivery," Lester mutters, his voice clipped and tense. His eyes flick to the side mirror, then the rearview, then back again. He hasn't stopped scanning since they passed the last checkpoint.

Dave gives him a sidelong glance. "You know you can't go in there, right? Your face is likely plastered on half the screens this side of the continent."

"I know," Lester admits, his jaw clenched. "But we need those components. There's no time to wait."

"How do you know this place has what you need?" Dave asks.

"We always had delivery crates brought to our lab. They came from all over the world. I just remember seeing this one and remembered it when you told me we were in Virginia," Lester replies.

Dave nods and his voice lowers, more earnest now. "Let me do it. I look like what I am—a delivery guy with a cheap hat and no ambition. No one's going to ask questions. You? You've got that hunted look. They'll sniff you out in seconds."

Lester considers the logic, then finally nods, exhaling through his nose. "Fine. Just be quick. Don't try to be a hero. If they catch on, bail."

Dave gives a quick salute with two fingers and pulls the truck off the main road, steering into a shadowed lot near a wide corrugated steel building with faded letters above the bay door: Tulber Inc. The name screams generic cover— exactly the kind of place Borvil would use for low-profile operations and supplies. Probably a subsidiary of Borvil itself.

The truck rumbles to a stop at a bay marked "Receiving." Dave kills the engine, its sudden silence almost jarring. He unbuckles his seatbelt, pauses, then glances at Lester one more time. "Just parts, right? Nothing flashy?"

Lester hesitates. "Xomithrine precursors. The kind Borvil likes to keep track of when their competition wants it too. The competition being Tericia and I."

Dave blinks. "As long as I don't have to know specifics, it's all good to me."

"Give me something to write on and I'll give you the list of items you'll need."

"Got it," Dave mutters. "Time to go pretend I know what the hell I'm doing."

He grabs a clipboard from the glove compartment—completely blank but scuffed enough to look official—hands it to Lester to make notes—takes the list and scans it over—and hops out of the truck as Lester gets into his hiding spot. Dave's boots crunch on the gravel as he walks to the entrance, past crates stacked haphazardly near the dock. The entrance sensor chirps softly, and the heavy steel door slides open with a hiss and groan, like it hasn't been maintained in years.

Inside, the air is cool and smells faintly of motor oil, metal shavings, ozone, and a whole host of other smells that are foreign to Dave. Bright lights buzz overhead, flickering like old nerves. Rows of high shelves tower over Dave as he steps in, each marked with codes and acronyms he doesn't understand.

At a desk near the entrance, a worker leans over a console, lazily tapping at keys. He doesn't even look up. "Delivery or pickup?"

"Pickup," Dave says with forced cheer. "Parts order. Should be under Borvil Corporation."

The man's fingers freeze mid-tap. Slowly, he lifts his gaze, narrowing his eyes at Dave like he's just mentioned a dirty word.

"Borvil, huh?" he repeats. "Don't see that one often." He types something, squinting at the screen. "Not seeing any record. Are you sure you're in the right place?"

Dave forces a shrug and steps closer. "They told me Tulber Inc. at this address. Said it was urgent—big project, top-down pressure, the usual circus. Maybe it's under a project code or acronym?"

The man scowls but starts typing again. "Nope. Not popping up."

Dave leans in slightly. "C'mon, man, I don't want to go back empty-handed. If I show up without this load, they'll have my ass on a platter. Look—here's the list."

He hands over the clipboard with a casual flick, praying the bluff holds. The worker snatches it, flipping through the handwritten sheets before nodding to himself. "Typical. Bastards never file things right. I mean, who even does handwritten things anymore. Follow me."

Dave tries not to sigh with relief as the worker motions for him to follow. They pass down three aisles of steel racking, each lined with labeled crates and sealed tubes. The man pulls items with practiced efficiency, stacking them on a wheeled flat cart: cylindrical containment units, sealed packets marked with radiation symbols, and a crate with reinforced clasps. They pile on bags of minerals and other dry chemicals. Stacks of solvents and carefully packaged wet chemicals. Equipment. The stack grows. Enough stuff to start a big chemistry lab. The cart becomes harder to maneuver. Eventually, they get everything on the list.

They round the last aisle when the worker suddenly stops, looks over his shoulder, and asks, "You're stealing this, aren't you?"

Dave freezes. His mouth opens but no words come out. His body language answers for him.

The worker smirks. "Relax. I don't care. Corporate doesn't pay me enough to be a snitch. Just…" he looks around, just to be sure, "remember me when you're rich and successful or making money selling this stuff or whatever the hell it is you're doing. Cut me in. I got a new baby on the way. Could really use the extra credits."

Dave exhales slowly, tension dripping from his shoulders. "Yeah. You'll get your cut. Name's Dave."

"Nathan," the worker replies, holding out a calloused hand.

They shake, and Nathan helps him load the parts into the back of the truck. As the final crate clunks into place, Nathan gives the door a solid slam. "Hope you know what you're doing."

"I really don't," Dave admits with a chuckle. "But it sounds cool, right?"

Nathan laughs. "Get outta here, weirdo."

Dave climbs back into the cab and presses the ignition button. The truck rumbles to life. He rolls away from the warehouse without speeding, without drawing a single eye. Once they've merged back onto the open road, he finally speaks.

"Safe to come out."

Lester's voice comes from under the seat. "Took your damn time."

Dave pops the latch and helps Lester unfold himself like an aging accordion. The scientist groans as he stretches, rubbing his neck and arms.

"I swear, another ten minutes and I'd have fused into a pretzel," Lester mutters. "So? How did it go?"

Dave gives a modest grin. "Smooth as synth-butter. Got everything we need. Made a new friend. Owe him a cut."

"You bribed a warehouse worker?" Lester blinks, incredulous.

"He bribed himself, really," Dave says. "I just didn't argue."

Lester lets out a surprised laugh, then sobers. "Good. That's good. Because we've got everything now— everything but Tericia. And I've got a feeling time's running out."

Dave looks over at him, hands steady on the wheel. "Then let's not waste any of it."

They drive on into the dark, the city fading behind them, the future waiting like an open wormhole—dangerous, uncertain, and full of possibility.

CHAPTER 32

"I guess you can only get so many tugs at a toenail before it just comes off," Tems mutters with a delighted chuckle, his cybernetic fingers masked by a layer of pliable carbon nano fiber. The pliers in his grip drip faintly with blood as he flings the torn nail across the room. Tericia's scream echoes through the metal walls, her body jerking in pain despite her restraints.

Her chest heaves, breaths ragged and shallow. The pain has gone from sharp to surreal—numb, like her mind is trying to protect itself from further damage. Still, she manages to grit her teeth and croak, "I thought... you got what you wanted from Nick."

Tems wipes his hands on a rag like a chef prepping for his next dish. "Oh, he gave us the cemetery location," he says casually. "But so far, it's been a big fat nothing. And well... let's just say that once you make a man watch his children die, he stops being cooperative." He shrugs like it's the most natural thing in the world.

"You sick fuck!" Tericia spits, fury barely giving way to her exhaustion.

Tems turns, eyes gleaming as he reaches for a new set of instruments. "Why? Because I do what's necessary? Because I don't let morality get in the way of victory?"

"They were just kids," she says through clenched teeth. "They didn't even have a choice. You didn't have to kill them."

"No," Tems replies, grabbing a lemon and a salt shaker from the tray beside him. "But that's what makes it effective. When you strip away hope, resistance collapses. Haven't you figured that out yet?" He walks back to her, slow and purposeful, as if savoring every step. "You've made this entertaining, Tericia. I always thought torture would be dull. But you? You've made it so fucking fun!"

He leans down and generously sprinkles salt on her newly exposed toe. The agony is immediate. Tericia's scream is inhuman—long, drawn out, raw. Her throat burns with it, her lungs gasping for air. Then Tems squeezes the lemon, letting juice drip slowly out of his cybernetic grip, watching how tightly he can squeeze it, taunting pain until it finally makes contact.

She convulses in the restraints, tears streaking down her face. "Why... why are you still doing this?" she pants, barely able to form the words.

"Because it's fun! I thought I already said that," Tems says, eyes wide with a manic glint, like a child holding a toy they never want to share. "And, well... you've still got information I want."

"You're... a disturbing—"

"Fuck?" Tems interrupts, grinning. "Please. You'd be the last person I'd fuck. Although..." His eyes drop to her groin, dark thoughts forming like storm clouds. "That does give me some good inspiration for what to try next."

"Stop!" Lester's shout breaks the calm of the cab. His hand slams against the dashboard, jolting Dave as the exit sign rushes toward them.

Dave swerves hard, the truck veering toward the final off-ramp before the border checkpoint. Tires squeal, horns blare behind them.

"Jesus, man!" Dave growls, gripping the wheel. "You wanna try giving me more than half a second next time?"

"Sorry. But we can't go over the border with this stuff," Lester says, eyes sharp with urgency. "Security will scan everything. They'll seize the components. Especially now. After that close call when we came over the border last time? You can bet Borvil has eyes on every crossing. Looking for anything out of the ordinary."

Dave exhales. "So, what do we do?"

"We process it here. Here in North Carolina," Lester replies. "Just enough fuel for two wormhole jumps. Then I can get to Tericia."

"You can hide that much in the compartment with you?" Dave asks, skeptical.

"I can try. Anything more, they'll catch. But two jumps is all we need if I don't screw it up."

Dave rubs his chin.

Lester continues, "Alright. We need a building. Abandoned. Isolated. Preferably not about to cave in. And if it blows up, we want no one around," Lester adds. "Because the process to create Xomithrine? It's not really safe. One wrong step and..." Lester doesn't say the word, he just demonstrates it with his hands.

"Where is the device?" Tems growls, pulling at Tericia's pants until they rip with a jagged tear. He leaves her exposed on the table, metal restraints biting into her skin. The blowtorch flares to life with a sharp hiss as he adjusts the flame, the heat casting a glow on the wall behind him.

"You don't... need to do this..." Tericia pleads, trembling—not from fear, but from the overwhelming adrenaline threatening to crash all at once.

Tems leans closer, torch in one hand, a red-hot steal rod in the other. "I don't need to. But I want to. You haven't exactly been cooperative."

"My pain must outweigh your need for that device," she says through gritted teeth. "So fuck you."

"Very well. More fun for me then," Tems sneers. He drops the torch, grabs the glowing rod with his cybernetic hand, and without hesitation, inserting it into her most vulnerable area.

The scream that tears from her throat is primal—pure agony incarnate. Her eyes roll back. Her muscles seize—and then she goes still.

Tems stares at her limp form, annoyed that she passed out. "Fuck!"

Dave pulls the truck into a deserted lot beside a crumbling warehouse, weeds snaking through cracked asphalt.

"I like to sleep in this parking lot when I am tired," he says. "Nobody comes around. Dead zone."

"Perfect," Lester mutters, hopping out of the cab. "Let's get moving."

Dave retrieves two pistols from under his seat. "I hate guns," he says. "But I've scared off more than a few tweakers with these."

"Bring them. We're going to need every advantage we can get," Lester demands, as he walks to the back and opens the truck.

"Where you takin' my stuff?" A man's voice creeps out from the darkness making Lester jump in his own skin, turning quickly to see a man with a knife and a shitty grin.

"I don't have time for this. Just fuck off and let me do what I need to do," Lester says loudly, hoping to tip off Dave that there is a new person joining the party.

"Oh yeah? And whatcha gotta do?" The man asks, moving the knife back and forth from one hand to the other with bravado.

"Science shit. Very dangerous. Likely to blow myself up. So, if you don't mind, I'd like to get to it and not deal with your stupid ass," Lester says, taunting the man as he climbs down from the back of the truck. "The love of my life is in danger, and I need to save her. Your knife doesn't scare me. Not after the ten years of torture I've been through."

"You are full of stories," the man says, moving closer, the knife leading the way.

Lester stands at the end of the truck. The man approaches and Lester holds onto the edge of the truck.

Dave appears behind the truck, eyes wide. Lester subtly shifts his gaze toward him.

The man catches the glance but misreads it—just long enough. Lester lunges forward, kicking the man in his groin. The knife clatters to the pavement. The man crumples with a wheeze.

"Gun!" Lester barks.

Dave tosses one. Lester catches it midair, spins, and fires. One shot. The man collapses, blood seeping into the concrete.

Dave stares, mouth slightly open. "You just... you shot him."

"Self-defense," Lester says, holstering the weapon with shaky hands. "I'll deal with the consequences later."

He turns to the crates. "Help me get this inside. We've got fuel to cook, and not a minute to spare. And Dave?"

"Yeah?"

"Start picking better parking lots to sleep in at night."

CHAPTER 33

"Wake up, you fucking bitch!" Tems growls, slapping Tericia across the face with the back of his hand. Her head jerks to the side, but she doesn't stir. Her body remains limp, her breath shallow. Passed out.

Tems snarls in frustration, pacing like a caged animal. "Guard! Get the fuck in here!"

The door opens and a young man in uniform steps through. He halts at the sight before him—Tericia, half-naked, strapped to the table, blood dripping from her toes, the now cooled metal rod still embedded between her legs. His expression falters for just a second.

Tems doesn't miss it. "Don't fucking stare. Just call me when she wakes up. I'm not wasting my time standing over her unconscious ass." He slams a communications device into the guard's hand.

"Yes, sir," the guard says quietly, stepping aside as Tems storms past him, slamming the door on his way out.

The room falls into an eerie silence. The guard, barely breathing, looks at the device for a moment, puts it in his back pocket, then walks over to the table and looks down at Tericia—at the wreckage Tems has left behind. He shakes his head slowly. "I didn't sign up for this shit."

He shifts his rifle to his back and leans in. With a quiet grunt, he grips the end of the metal rod. It doesn't move easily—fused to the tissue, burned into the muscle. He doesn't hesitate. He pulls. The rod slides free with a sickening sound, tearing more than just flesh on its way out.

She moans faintly, still unconscious.

The guard moves quickly, silently. He digs through drawers, finds a set of scrubs, and carefully threads her legs into the pants. Then gauze. Bandages. Makeshift field dressing on her mangled toes. He moves to the restraints and undoes them one by one, catching her before she slumps.

He lifts her gently and carries her out of the room, down the corridor toward the rear exit. Outside, under dim security lights, he lays her carefully into the passenger seat of his old corporate-issued sedan and straps her in.

Then he runs back inside, eyes scanning every room and cabinet. "I know she came here for something," he mutters. "Come on. What the hell is Xomithrine? What kind of container is it in?"

Drawer after drawer. Shelf after shelf. He opens everything that isn't nailed shut. But nothing jumps out.

He gives up and sprints back out the rear exit—only to freeze.

The passenger door is wide open. The seat empty. The shotgun missing.

"Shit," he hisses, spinning around looking for any sigh of her. "Hey! I'm trying to help you!" His voice echoes through the night. "I didn't fucking sign up for this either!"

Movement.

He catches the glint of a barrel in the dark. A shotgun pointed straight at his face.

He stops. Raises his hands. Tericia stands before him, blood-smeared, hair damp with sweat, barely able to stay upright—but her grip on the weapon is steady.

"And I'm supposed to believe you?" she rasps, voice hollow from pain, but sharp with fury.

"I bandaged you. I pulled that fucking thing out. I brought you clothes," he says, slow and even. "Tems left. Told me to call him when you came to. I didn't. I haven't. I brought you out here instead. We need to get you medical help."

She doesn't lower the weapon. "Why? Why risk your ass for me?"

"Because that… that shit in there wasn't war. That was a fucking horror show," he says, pointing back toward the building. "I've been with Tems a year. I've seen shit. But not like that. He's ruthless and I don't like it."

"Why keep doing it?" Tericia asks bluntly.

"The pay is good and I am pretty sure resigning might come with some unintended consequences," the guard replies.

"Yeah. My colleagues met the same end. Death. So, yes, you would meet an unfortunate end if you tried to quit," Tericia shares.

He nods. "Yeah. Which is why I'm not quitting. I'm switching sides."

They stare at each other a beat longer.

Then, Tericia nods slowly. "I need Xomithrine. I know it's here somewhere."

He turns, and they move back inside together. "I looked, but didn't find any. Although, truth be told, I don't know what I am looking for."

Tericia nods.

"Name?" she asks.

"Ralph."

"Tericia."

She leads him through a narrow corridor, slow, shuffling her feet more than taking large strides, stopping in front of a door with faded red stenciling: EXTREME DANGER.

"Open it," she says.

Ralph hesitates, glancing at her. "What's in there?"

"The only thing that matters. Just don't touch anything I don't tell you to. Seriously. One wrong bump and we both go up like fireworks on a fucking holiday."

Gulping, he opens the door slowly and steps inside. The air is colder here. Sterile. The hum of equipment buzzes low and ominous.

"Look for long, skinny blue cylinders," she instructs. "They'll have a symbol—XoMr. That's the compound."

Ralph keeps his rifle tight to his back and tucks his hands close. He navigates between tightly packed shelves until finally—"Got one!"

He lifts a blue canister and carries it back toward her.

Tericia nods. "That's it. Perfect."

"How many do we need?"

"All of them."

Ralph glances back toward the shelves. "There are at least twenty."

"Then get moving. I'll take this one out to the car."

"No—wait—" He tries to stop her, but she's already gone.

Ralph hurries back in to grab another.

Tericia limps down the corridor, dragging the canister, every step painting the floor with blood. Her legs tremble. Her vision blurs. She stumbles once, catches herself on the wall, gasping through clenched teeth.

The exit is just ahead.

She pushes through the door, into the open night, and collapses. The cylinder rolls out of her hands as her body hits the pavement hard. Her head lolls to the side, eyes fluttering closed as the pain finally overwhelms her.

Darkness takes her.

And the canister lies beside her, waiting.

CHAPTER 34

Dave and Lester load the Xomithrine canisters beneath Lester's seat, the containers sliding into place with a heavy clunk. Lester does his best to pad the area so the canisters don't jostle around during the trip. Once confident in his setup, Lester wipes his hands on his pants, already anxious.

"Let's move," he says, sliding into the passenger seat. "I don't know how much longer Tericia has. The longer she's gone, the worse it's going to be."

Dave throws the truck into gear, glancing sideways. "We floor it, we get flagged. Flash one wrong signal and the whole system lights up. Let me do what I do best."

Lester exhales through his nose, barely hiding his impatience. "Just say the word when it's time to disappear. No hesitation."

Dave smirks, shifting smoothly into traffic. "Good. Because out here, efficiency isn't just smart—it's survival."

The truck rumbles forward, engine low and steady, disappearing into the blur of road ahead.

Tericia blinks through the fog, her vision swimming as streaks of light slip past the windows. The motion turns her stomach. Her tongue scrapes across the dry roof of her mouth. Her head throbs, the pulsing behind her eyes warning just how dehydrated she is.

Shapes blur until one settles: Ralph.

"There she is," he says with a relieved grin. "Had me worried for a second."

He hands her a bottle of water, the cap already twisted open. "Drink."

She takes it, sips slow. Her lips crack from the motion. "Where are we? Where are we going?"

"Just crossed into Virginia," Ralph says, hands tight on the wheel. "I overheard them... that family. Begging. Pleading..." He doesn't finish the sentence. His jaw clenches, eyes staring ahead like he's afraid they might betray how shaken he is.

"They didn't deserve that," Tericia mutters. Her voice is gravel.

"No. They didn't." Ralph swallows hard. "That's why I'm helping you. Instead of that evil... that—"

"Fuck," she says for him. "Call him what he is."

He nods slowly. "Yeah. That."

"He'll get what's coming to him," she says, her tone low, deliberate. "I've got a plan. One he won't see coming." Her eyes narrow. "Did they tell you which cemetery?"

"Yeah. They gave a name. Fairmonte Cemetery. With a mausoleum location." Ralph glances over. "We sent a whole damn team, couldn't find anything."

Tericia's brow furrows. "Fairmonte?" Her voice sharpens. "They both said that?"

"Just Nick," Ralph says. "His wife and kids stayed silent. No one bothered to ask her if it was a lie."

Tericia exhales through a cracked smile, leaning her head back. "Good for him. And them. Holding the line even when everything's burning."

Ralph squints. "So that wasn't the right place?"

"Nope," Tericia says with a smile that cracks her lips even further.

"Well... where the hell am I taking you then?"

"Head toward highway 460. We need to get near Bedford," she says, taking another gulp of water, wincing at the way it hits her stomach. "Wake me when we're close."

"You could just tell me the cemetery name. I'll handle the rest."

She doesn't answer. Just gives him a smile that says *not a chance in hell*, and lets herself drift back into the dark.

"It's time. Get under the seat," Dave says, eyes locked on the green highway sign announcing the state line.

Without a word, he pops the seat. Lester unfolds the hidden compartment, then climbs in like he's done it a dozen times—though the grunt that escapes him as he wrangles the Xomithrine containers around his torso betrays the pain.

"Jesus. It's tighter than before," Lester mutters, curling into himself, his knees pressed against the metal.

"You ready?" Dave asks, hand poised to shut the lid.

"No. But do it anyway," Lester growls.

Dave smirks and slams the seat shut. The cab falls silent.

He eases the truck toward the border, keeping his speed steady. Calm. No sudden movements. The surveillance towers loom ahead, dull eyes blinking red. Dave keeps his hands at ten and two, heart steady.

They roll past the checkpoint. Cameras pivot. Scanners ping. Nothing stops them.

He exhales. "We're through... but don't celebrate just yet," Dave mutters under his breath. "They stopped me heading out. Could happen again. Protocol bullshit."

From under the seat, muffled and strained, Lester hisses, "Fuck!"

Dave doesn't respond. He just keeps driving, jaw tight, knuckles white on the wheel. A small smirk growing on his face, living his dream, feeling the adrenaline.

"We're in Bedford," Ralph says, nudging Tericia awake with the back of his hand.

She jerks in place, blinking through the haze. The city rolls past the windows—streetlights, old brick buildings, a rusted water tower in the distance. It takes her a few seconds to orient herself.

"I said wake me when we were close, not inside the goddamn city," she mutters, squinting at the passing signs. "Now we'll have to backtrack."

"Sorry," Ralph says with a shrug. "You looked like you needed the sleep."

Tericia doesn't argue. Her body feels like it's made of broken glass. She shifts in the seat, then glances down at herself—at the blood-soaked gauze between her legs. "We need to stop. Somewhere discreet."

"Yeah," Ralph nods, eyes flicking to the same place she just looked.

"And food. And water. My mouth feels like I swallowed sandpaper."

Ralph doesn't respond—just merges onto a side street and pulls into the back lot of a run-down convenience store. The parking lot is empty. One flickering light overhead buzzes like it's ready to die.

"No one messes with me when I'm in this car," Ralph says.

"I wonder why," Tericia snaps, her voice edged with sarcasm. "Borvil's got their filthy hands on everything. Everyone's been fucked by them one way or another."

Ralph kills the engine. Silence settles over the car. He opens his door.

Tericia moves slowly, reaching for her own handle. Her stomach flips. Her head swims. Nausea claws at her throat.

Ralph walks around to help her out—just as she was hoping he would.

As she slides out, her hand moves fast. The knife she palmed from the glovebox flashes from her sleeve and drives deep into Ralph's gut.

"What the fuck!?" Ralph staggers back, eyes wide, the knife still lodged in him. Blood seeps through his shirt.

"You've been acting off," Tericia growls, stepping forward. Her voice shakes with pain, but her grip is steady. "Something about the escape, the way you 'just happened' to be around, the fact that you never questioned where we were going until we got close, we weren't followed, contacted by Tems, told to deviate... it all felt too easy."

"I wasn't—" Ralph gasps, clutching the wound. "I wasn't lying to you..."

"You kept your hand on your gun the whole fucking ride," Tericia snaps, stepping closer. "That's not helping your case."

Ralph slowly lifts his hand away from the holster, breathing hard, eyes pleading.

Tericia reaches in and pulls the knife out. Her hand trembles—but she hides it. She's not about to show weakness now.

"I really am..." Ralph chokes, coughing blood.

"A fucking Borvil lackey," she says coldly.

She jams the knife between his ribs and drives it deep. He shudders, collapsing to his knees, gurgling as blood fills his lungs.

Tericia doesn't flinch. She rips the keys from his belt as he crumples to the ground. No more second chances. No more maybe-this-time.

The device slinks from his pocket and falls to the ground, Tericia can see the words clearly, 'Be convincing.'

She gets in the truck, slams the door, and guns it out of the lot—tires screeching as she cuts south through the streets of Bedford.

Dave and Lester pull into the cemetery, gravel crunching beneath the tires as they coast past rows of worn tombstones. It's quiet—too quiet—and Lester's pulse picks up as they near the mausoleum. His eyes, jutting around, looking for the danger he senses.

"Leave the truck here," Lester says, climbing out and grabbing the container of Xomithrine from the floor. "Looks like a delivery. Less suspicious."

Dave hops out behind him with the other canister, his eyes wide with boyish excitement. "This is better than I imagined. Like, way better. We're walking into secret bunker shit here, right?"

Lester doesn't respond. He's too focused, too on edge. He starts walking with Dave struggling to keep up. They're halfway down the main cemetery road when the squeal of tires cuts through the silence like a gunshot.

A car rips into the cemetery at full speed, fishtailing across the loose gravel and swerving between headstones.

Lester freezes. "Fuck!" His eyes dart left, right—nothing but tombstones, no cover. He drops the Xomithrine and yanks out his pistol.

Dave skids to a halt beside him. "What? What is it?"

"Borvil," Lester growls. "How the fuck did they find us?"

The car screams to a stop, dirt and dust curling into the air. The doors burst open—and then Lester sees her.

Tericia.

Eyes wide. Limping. Bleeding. Bandaged feet. A gun raised.

Lester's finger tenses on the trigger, an instant away from pulling, but then lowered with gratification of seeing her.

Tericia sees him.

Then she sees Dave.

Her pistol pivots with precision, now aimed at Dave's head. "Who the fuck is this?" she snarls, limping forward with fire in her eyes.

Dave throws up his hands. "Whoa! WHOA! Hey—!"

Lester steps between them fast, blocking her line of fire. "He's with me! I hijacked his truck—he's been helping me since. He's clean."

Tericia doesn't lower her weapon. "You check him for a tracker? A wire? Anything?"

"He's not wired."

"That's not a fucking answer, Lester."

Lester moves in closer, puts a hand on her shoulder, sees the pain she's barely holding together. Her body's shaking, but she's still aiming steady. "Love," he says softly, "do you trust me?"

Her eyes flick to his. Bloodshot. Exhausted. Burning. "I trust you. I don't trust him."

"Then trust that I trust him," Lester says. His voice is solid. Final. "Please."

Tericia's breathing starts to slow. Her arm lowers slightly— but only slightly. Her face starts to slacken. "But… we were… so… close…"

Her knees buckle.

Lester catches her just as she falls.

"Shit—Tericia—hey!" he cradles her, lifting her gently as her eyes roll back and her head slumps against his chest.

Dave stands frozen, hands still up, face pale. "Is she—?"

"She's alive," Lester breathes, holding her tight. "But barely."

He looks down at the blood soaking through her makeshift bandages. Then back at Dave.

"Help me get her and the Xomithrine inside. We're out of time."

CHAPTER 35

Tericia blinks hard, trying to push through the fog clouding her vision. The light above pulses like a heartbeat, cold and clinical. She turns her head slowly, eyes landing on the sterile white walls of the medical room. She's back in the bunker. Back where it finally felt safe. Machines hum around her, scanning and repairing, their soft whir a lullaby to her trauma.

She wiggles her toes. They respond. No stabbing pain. No raw agony. Just movement. Her fingers flex next, and then—cautiously—she slowly tightens her pelvic muscles. No flare of white-hot pain. No burning reminder of Tems. She tries again, harder this time. Still nothing. Relief, heavy and silent, settles across her like a weighted blanket. But it doesn't last.

She shifts, and the machine beeps in protest.

Lester jolts upright in his chair beside her, still half-asleep, his hand instinctively moving toward the control panel. His gaze lands on her. For a second, he freezes—caught between disbelief and overwhelming relief.

Tericia meets his eyes. They hold each other's gaze like it's the only thing tethering them to reality. A shared smile flickers through the exhaustion.

"What the—" they both say at the same time.

Lester gestures for her to go first.

"What the fuck were you doing out there? And with some random guy named... umm..."

"Dave," Lester says, scratching the back of his neck. "You didn't come back. I didn't know if you were dead or worse. I figured I'd need to make Xomithrine on my own if I was going to find you. Dave was just some truck driver who pulled into the cemetery at the wrong time. Turns out the guy's always dreamed of being a fugitive." Lester leaves out the part where he was hired to be there, knowing it would just cause more arguments and frustrations than is worth it.

Tericia raises a brow. "Oh. Well, shit. Still, you shouldn't have left the bunker."

"Parmen stayed behind to guard it," Lester reminds her gently. Then, his voice shifts. "Speaking of left... where's Nick? His family?"

The silence hits like a gunshot.

Tericia lowers her gaze, her hands threading through her hair as she exhales hard.

"Borvil?" Lester's voice is sharp. Jaw clenched.

"Tems, actually," Tericia admits, slightly nodding to the reality.

"Wait! What!? He's not dead?" Lester asks, confusion racing, his mind trying to find an answer as to how Tems survived.

"He's not. And he now has a cybernetic arm and leg," Tericia says as she moves her jaw around, reminded of how strong his grip is.

"He the one who did... all of it?" Lester asks, his anger raging inside.

Another nod. Slower this time. Shame, rage, and grief wrapped around her like a straitjacket.

"How'd you get out?" Lester pushes. "And please—tell me he's dead. Tell me we don't have to see him ever again."

"Oh, he's dead," Tericia says, her voice low and sharp as shattered glass. Her eyes meet his again, and this time they burn. "He just doesn't know it yet."

She doesn't wait for a response. She rips the monitors off her body, pushes away the machines. Naked, trembling, furious—she swings her legs over the bed.

"Wait, wait—what did he do? How did you get out?" Lester asks, following her.

"He thought he was smarter than me," Tericia snarls, bolting into the hallway. "Had a guard pretend to care. Pretend to help. Pretend to—fuck!"

"What?" Lester asks, wanting to know more.

"Where are the canisters I brought?" Tericia asks, her eyes issuing a need for an expedited response.

"Down by Holepunch," Lester replies quickly.

She storms out of the room and down the stairs, past the empty halls, past Parmen's room, past Holepunch's threshold. She drops to her knees at the Xomithrine containers. One by one, she pries them open.

Sand.

Fucking sand.

And inside—small blinking tracking devices.

"FUCK!" she screams, slamming one container into the wall. It explodes into a spray of sand and shattered metal. "Fuck! Fuck! We need to leave now! He played me—he fucking played me!"

Lester rushes in just as she cracks the next container. Same contents. He doesn't ask—he knows. "I'll get the others."

"No need," says Parmen, voice flat as he appears in the doorway. Dave trails behind him, eyes wide as dinner plates.

"Whoa," Dave mutters, spotting Tericia naked and raging. "Wow."

"Dave!" Lester shouts, stepping in front of her.

"Sorry," Dave mutters. "Been a while..."

"Clothes. Now!" Lester orders.

Dave nods and bolts up the stairs.

"I managed to synthesize more," Lester says. "We've got just enough for two jumps. One of them's got to be to a Xomithrine facility. Or we're fucked."

The entire room lurches like it's been punched by God.

"Explosion," Parmen growls, weapon already half-raised. "That had to be the mausoleum. They're here."

"Motherfucker," Tericia hisses, scrambling for the console. Fingers flying. Coordinates punching through the air. Dave returns, tossing clothes to Lester, who helps her dress while she codes.

"Hurry!" Parmen shouts from the door. "They're coming down the access ramps."

Tericia slams her palm on the panel. The wormhole roars to life, blue and furious.

"Go!" she screams.

Parmen dives through. Dave hesitates just a second—long enough to look at Lester, then vanishes into the wormhole. Lester hands Tericia the rest of her clothes, then leaps after them.

The inner door explodes.

Tericia turns at the sound—dust, fire, and shadow flooding the hallway. Armed boots pounding closer.

She smiles, half-healed and defiant, and pushes the device forward with her last strength. The wormhole swallows her just as the armed soldiers get to the door to overtake the room.

The wormhole slams shut behind her.

CHAPTER 36

"That was so cool!" Dave shouts, eyes wild with exhilaration as the group stands on solid ground again, the wormhole snapping shut behind them.

"Where are we now?" he asks, looking around the dim, sterile walls.

Lester scans the familiar surroundings, his stomach sinking. "The last place I ever wanted to come back to," he mutters, each word laced with regret.

"No," Tericia says flatly, locking eyes with him. "The last place he would expect us to come."

Lester's brows knit together. "And you think there's just... extra Xomithrine lying around?"

"We don't have time for doubt. Let's find some—fast," Tericia says, motioning to Dave and Parmen.

Lester's jaw tightens. "Yeah. Let's."

Tericia freezes. "What is your fucking problem?"

"I nearly died trying to get that fuel so I could save you," Lester snaps, voice rising. "You nearly died on the damn table, and now you've put us in the heart of Borvil's hornet's nest. This place is drenched in surveillance— we're probably already on camera. I'm surprised we aren't already dead."

Parmen raises a hand like a ref in a bar fight. "If you two are done biting each other's throats out, maybe we can, I dunno, not die here?"

"Yes. Maybe we can," Tericia says, holding Lester's gaze a beat longer before storming toward the old storage room.

Lester rolls his eyes and starts to follow Tericia.

"Why aren't you looking elsewhere?" Tericia asks as she notices Lester following her.

"We were here for 10 years. It was never anywhere else. Why would I look elsewhere?" Lester asks in a tone that suggests Tericia is stupid for asking.

"Fuck you," she spits over her shoulder.

"What the fuck are you even mad at me for?" Lester barks as Tericia kicks the door open hard enough to nearly rip it off the hinges, ignoring Lester's question completely.

The overhead light flickers to life, casting a cold eerie glow over the shelves.

And there it is.

Stacked Xomithrine canisters—untouched, just like they left them.

Tericia strides forward, her tone snapping back into command mode. "Check for trackers before we take anything."

"Oh, come on. Of course they're tracked. 'We don't take chances,' remember?" Lester mutters as he joins her.

"Then we strip them, transfer the contents, and burn the containers," she fires back. "We don't exactly have a luxury of options."

"Seriously," Lester asks, stepping closer. "What did I do to deserve all this fury from you?"

She goes still. The silence swells between them. Anger boiling inside of her. Lester hesitates, then places a gentle hand on her shoulder. She shrugs it off.

He wraps his arms around her anyway.

She stiffens. Then breaks.

The sobs come like a wave crashing over a dam. Guttural, raw, unstoppable. Her body shakes in his arms as the pain she's kept locked away for days—years—erupts out of her.

Lester holds her tighter, saying nothing, just being the wall she can fall against.

Parmen and Dave appear at the doorway. Lester makes eye contact and gives them a subtle nod toward the shelves. Quietly, they begin grabbing containers.

"Talk to me," Lester whispers.

Tericia gasps between sobs. "I failed. I almost got us all killed. I got Nick... his wife... I got his kids killed. I've gotten so many people..."

"No," Lester cuts in sharply. "No. You don't get to wear that shit. Tems did that. He made those choices. Not you."

"I left you behind to keep you safe," she says, pulling back enough to meet his eyes. "And you left. You put yourself in danger. For what? For me? I don't deserve that."

"Yes you do. And now you know how I felt when you left. Scared I would never see you again," Lester says with a small grin. "But it worked out. We're here. We're alive."

She wipes her face with her sleeve. "I'm just tired. Tired of fighting. I just want to go back to that planet and be a fucking scientist again."

"Then let's finish Tems. Burn Borvil to the ground. Wipe out every wormhole device but ours," Lester replies, lifting her chin. "But we can't do that if we're busy tearing each other apart."

She nods slowly. "You're right. I get it."

"Guys," Parmen calls, tension coiled in his voice. "I don't want to alarm you, but we need to leave. Like now. I don't know how to work your device, and I hear company gathering fast on the other side of the door over there."

"Shit," Tericia mutters, already sprinting toward Holepunch.

Parmen draws his gun and plants himself between the team and the door.

"Where do I stand?" Dave blurts, ducking and spinning in place. "This is so not my usual Tuesday."

The door slams open with a thunderous crack. A storm of boots rushes in as Holepunch begins to hum. The soldiers unleash their weapons.

Tericia types in coordinates. Lights flicker and the wormhole tears open in front of Parmen, sucking in bullets that were meant for his flesh.

"Take the containers through. Then move aside before they shoot you in the back," Tericia commands.

Dave doesn't need to be told twice. He barrels through the wormhole, arms full. Parmen follows, then Lester grabs the remaining cases.

"Go!" Tericia yells.

"Together," Lester says, grabbing her hand and Holepunch simultaneously. They push it through just as another explosion shakes the room. The wormhole seals shut behind them.

They land in a heap. Lester wraps his arms around her as they catch their breath.

"Now what?" Dave says, already up and pacing.

Tericia groans.

Lester blinks, then perks up. "Get more containers—any that look like the ones we used, but different colors."

"What for?" Dave asks.

"So we know which containers are bugged and which ones aren't," Tericia explains. "We need to ditch the trackers."

"I have an idea," Lester says.

Tericia squints. "Well?"

"I'll show you once we are ready," Lester exclaims, a smile growing on his face.

The group finds similar containers and some additional hardware that allows them to attach those containers to Holepunch for an easy storage solution. They transfer the

Xomithrine to the new containers and notice the tracking bugs at the bottom of each Borvil container.

"Okay. Now, what is your plan?" Tericia asks.

"Since we have a lot of Xomithrine now, I suggest we send Borvil on a wild goose chase. We open wormholes to as many different places as there are containers. We send one through each…"

"And they are left tracking each container, spending time and resources, not finding anything," Tericia finishes Lester's thoughts.

"And then, that gives us more time to find a new place to hide, and a place to store Xomithrine. Once we find a place, we just gather all known supplies for our own use," Lester shares. "Finally giving us the upper hand."

"I love it!" Tericia declares, standing by Holepunch. She starts putting in coordinates for the first bugged container. A smile taking hold.

CHAPTER 37

"That's the last one," Tericia says, sealing the wormhole with a final, solid press of the panel. The swirling blue light fizzles into nothingness. "Now it's time to find a home base. A place to store the Xomithrine. A place to mount our assault on Tems and the entire corrupt rot that is the Borvil Corporation."

Lester exhales slowly, setting the last crate aside. "I've been thinking… maybe we take it all to that planet Parmen found."

"I like that idea!" Dave and Parmen blurt out in unison— Dave with the giddy excitement of a sci-fi fanboy, Parmen with the focused resolve of a soldier.

Tericia shoots them all a warning glance. "Need I remind you? Borvil already has access to that planet. For all we know, they've dropped a team there by now. We have no intel, no resources mapped, no guarantees."

"But anywhere we go, we have options. We can go anywhere to get what we need and have the fuel to do it," Lester counters. "If we move all the Xomithrine there and destroy any wormhole devices that link back to it, Borvil loses their foothold. We know where that interim wormhole device sits. We can just go there and destroy them as often as they get placed. That gives us the edge."

"And with this device," he adds, motioning to the wormhole generator, "we can grab anything we need. Ships. Weapons. Fuel. Fucking canned peaches if it comes to that."

Tericia studies him, then Dave and Parmen. She sighs, long and tired. "No exploring. Not until we're safe. Not until we know they're not tracking us. Not until we know they can never get to that planet without us."

"I promise," Lester says, his voice low but steady.

"The mission first!" Parmen adds in his best drill-sergeant voice.

"I can't make that promise," Dave grins, hands raised in surrender.

Tericia rolls her eyes but smirks. "Fine. Let's go find a place to call home."

She types in the coordinates for the planet Parmen had jokingly dubbed Planet Vista. The wormhole opens with a familiar pulse of blue light.

"Planet Vista! Here we come!" Parmen hollers, marching through like he owns the place.

"You do realize the people who lived there already had a name for it, right?" Lester says, giving Parmen a playful slap on the shoulder.

"Whatever. If they come back they can tell me all about it," Parmen shrugs, vanishing through the wormhole.

The others follow.

They step through into a towering structure at the heart of the alien city. Unlike last time, this puts them inside the tallest building they had previously observed from a distance. The room is vast, its walls lined with strange geometric patterns glowing faintly under the dim alien light.

Dust lies thick on the floor, but the windows give a panoramic view of the sprawling alien cityscape below.

The city stretches out in all directions. Towering spires twist into the skies like the bones of a long-dead civilization. Streets curve at unnatural angles, covered in strange vegetation and crumbling vehicles frozen mid-abandonment. Massive, domed buildings loom on the outskirts, cracked and covered in vines. It's like humanity's mirror image, warped by time and distance.

"This place is massive," Dave whispers. "But where the hell is everyone?"

"Let's find out later," Tericia says. "Right now, we need to know what supplies we have and then get the supplies we need. Food. Water. As much fuel as we can find. Maybe additional wormhole device components."

"On it," Parmen says, already moving. "We'll check the rest of this level."

They split up. Parmen finds what looks like a lounge space. Dave stumbles into a kitchen-like area, complete with weird metallic cabinets and long counters. Lester locates what might be storage rooms and even an old bathroom setup.

A few minutes later, they reconvene.

"This whole floor's set up like it was meant for people like us," Parmen says.

"It's… uncanny. Too human to not be human," Tericia mutters. "We'll need to study that later."

"No time like the present," Lester says, hopeful that they can skip taking on Borvil.

"Nope. First, supply run." Tericia opens a wormhole to a bulk warehouse store in a location that is now after hours. Emergency lights flicker overhead. The warehouse is quiet—closed to the public, dim in nature, hard to see everything.

"We're going in?" Dave asks.

"Not all of us," Tericia says. "Someone has to stay behind to reopen the wormhole in case it closes. The coordinates are set, so if it does close, just wait five minutes and reopen to the same spot."

She points to the controls and walks everyone through how to reopen the same coordinates. Everyone nods.

Tericia stays while the guys go through and return a few minutes later, huffing and puffing, lugging heavy packages filled with bottled water.

They make run after run, piling hundreds of packs of bottled water into the lounge space. Then come food runs—protein bars, jerky, canned goods, nuts. Junk food. Anything with shelf life.

Sweating and out of breath, Dave drops his latest load and wipes his forehead. "Fuck me, I haven't worked this hard since my last gym membership expired."

"Where's Parmen?" Tericia asks.

Lester and Dave shrug.

"I'll go find him," Tericia says, grabbing her gun.

She steps through the wormhole into the warehouse's stale air. The buzzing of distant lights fills her ears. She hears boots clomping, metal clanging, something rolling—too much noise to ignore. Her heart rate spikes. Her hands shake. She squeezes the grip on her gun and presses forward, moving between shelves stacked high with product.

Focus, she tells herself.

A loud crash yanks her attention to the left. She ducks behind a row of stacked crates and raises her weapon.

'Should I call out? Or would that draw attention to me?' Tericia asks herself. 'Best to remain silent.'

Then—motion.

Before Tericia can gather her thoughts, Parmen barrels into view, pushing a huge cart stacked with food, batteries, solar lights, even fucking dishes.

"Fuck!" Tericia lowers her weapon. "You scared the shit out of me."

Parmen grins. "Found the jackpot."

He shoves the cart through the wormhole without hesitation. "Mattresses next. I saw a whole bunch of them back there."

Tericia nods, helping Parmen get the items through. "Yeah. Let's not sleep on cold floors."

Soon, the three men return carrying mattresses—Parmen and Dave with twins, Lester with something larger.

He smiles as he steps through. "Figured we'd want to be comfortable."

Tericia smiles back.

The wormhole closes with a final shimmer when Tericia decides they have enough.

They look at their stockpile—water, food, gear, mattresses.

"Well?" Dave asks, hands on his hips.

Tericia sighs, exhaustion washing over her. "Let's get some goddamn sleep. We earned it."

They laugh. And for the first time in a long time, it almost feels like the start of something normal.

CHAPTER 38

Tericia blinks herself awake, eyelids heavy but her body... calm. For the first time in what feels like years, she doesn't wake in a panic, doesn't jolt upright expecting to see blood, chains, or the blank stare of a dead friend. No sirens, no screaming, no dread crawling under her skin like an itch she can't scratch. Just quiet.

She lies still for a moment, letting the strange calm sink in. Her breath rises soft beneath the thin blanket. She glances to her side.

The bed is empty.

Lester's missing.

She groans softly, wraps the blanket tighter around her shoulders, and pads barefoot into the main room, her body still stiff from torture, battle, sleep, and a what feels like a hundred years of tension clenching her bones.

Lester stands by the window, arms crossed, eyes fixed on the horizon of the alien cityscape. Tall structures rise like monoliths against the sky—angular, clean, sturdy. Wind brushes past the exterior, but inside the room, all is still.

Tericia joins him, her shoulder brushing his. Together, they gaze out the glass.

"I don't think this civilization's been gone long," Lester says quietly, like he's afraid to disturb the ghosts that might still linger. "Not much overgrowth. Little decay. The buildings are solid. Mass extinction maybe?"

"I don't think they died. I think they left," Tericia murmurs.

Lester turns to her, brow furrowed. "Left? What makes you say that?"

"Have you seen a single body?"

Lester blinks. "No. But we haven't exactly searched every floor."

She shrugs. "No signs of panic. No rot. No bones."

"Maybe the few survivors relocated. Or maybe it wasn't a mass extinction thing—maybe it was a migration."

"Maybe." Her voice is distant. "We don't have nearly enough to know anything for certain."

The door creaks behind them.

"You two wanna keep it down?" Dave mumbles with a sleepy grin, stepping into the room, rubbing his eyes. "Some of us are still pretending this is a vacation."

Tericia and Lester glance at each other. Dave ambles toward the window, then stops short, squinting.

"Hey… shouldn't we be alone on this planet?"

Lester's brows narrow. "What?"

Dave points out the window. "There. Down on the main path."

Lester and Tericia move closer, pressing up to the glass. Below, a group of men in uniform walks with purpose. Tactical vests. Boots. Weapons. Data tablets.

"Borvil?" Lester whispers.

"Looks like it," Tericia mutters. "It's their uniform colors."

"Go get Parmen. Now," Lester says.

Dave doesn't hesitate. He bolts.

Tericia and Lester stay locked on the patrol. Two men at the rear stop, pointing at a nearby structure and scribbling on their tablets.

"What do we do?" Lester asks, his voice tight.

"We knew they had access," Tericia says. "They're probably scouting. Planning something."

"For what? Why the hell would Borvil care about this place now?"

"Profit." She spits the word like a curse. "They'll turn this whole city into a luxury frontier experience. A resort on a new world. Charge assholes a million credits to hike an alien jungle and drink overpriced purified water."

She taps the glass. "Those two in the back? Those are analysts. They're assessing value. Or where to build. Or something like that."

Footsteps echo behind them.

"What's going on?" Parmen yawns as he enters the room.

"We've got company," Lester says, waving him over.

Parmen peers out, takes one look, and immediately hardens. "We need weapons."

"Fuel first," Tericia snaps. "We burned a ton opening portals and sending decoys."

"How many jumps left?" Parmen asks.

Tericia checks Holepunch. "Maybe three more."

"Anywhere that has weapons and Xomithrine?" Parmen asks, scanning the room for his gear.

She and Lester share a look.

"Military outposts?" Parmen suggests.

Tericia shrugs. "Maybe. But anything that might contain Xomithrine is likely to be a trap, or bugged, under surveillance. You know how it is."

"Then we get weapons first," Parmen says. "If it's a trap, we're not showing up empty-handed."

Lester nods. "I can take us back to where I synthesized Xomithrine. There's still enough for a couple refuels."

"That's two trips then," Parmen says, watching the patrol vanish behind a distant building. "And if they didn't spot us yet, we keep it that way."

Tericia sniffs the air, then grimaces. "Also, clothes. We reek."

They all pause, then collectively realize they smell like war, sweat, and stale exhaustion.

"Where to Parmen? Pick a depot," Tericia says, stepping to the controls.

The wormhole opens to the inside of what looks like an abandoned barn, its walls weathered and crooked. Dust filters through wooden slats. Sand curls along the floor in lazy dunes.

"The African front. An old weapons depot from the Prontic War," Parmen says as he steps through. "They thought they'd fight on this continent but never did. So they left it. A few outcast guards stuck around to keep it off the books."

He steps in fully, scanning the darkness with his gun raised.

Dave follows, wide-eyed and breathing fast. Lester moves in behind him, keeping low.

They fan out, grabbing what they can—rifles, laser pistols, EMP grenades, ammo crates, vests. Dave finds a rack of tactical gear and starts suiting up like a kid in a costume store.

Lester returns through the wormhole and hands Tericia a sleek pulse rifle. "Cover us. I don't want a repeat of last time."

Tericia smirks, grips the weapon, and shoulders it. "Go. I've got your backs."

Trip after trip, the gear piles high back in their safehouse. Everything they could want—short of a full army.

Parmen is the last to step through. He's loaded head to toe—combat armor, grenades strapped to his thighs, a rifle in each hand, and a rocket launcher slung across his back.

"Close it," he says.

Tericia shuts down the wormhole, the blue shimmer collapsing into silence.

"That went smoothly," she says. "Nice to have a win for once."

"Hey guys?" Dave says, standing at the window.

Everyone turns.

"Who the fuck is that?"

They all rush to the window.

And there, at the edge of the square below, stands a single figure.

Not in uniform. Not moving.

Just watching.

CHAPTER 39

"Don't panic. Don't panic," Tericia whispers under her breath, trying to reassure herself and stave off the PTSD.

"Who are you talking to?" Lester asks, eyes narrowing.

"Myself." Her voice is flat, eyes locked on the figure below. "That guy is like a fucking cancer."

"We've got weapons," Parmen says, steady, calculating. "We could take him out now—he's vulnerable. Probably the best chance we'll get."

"And if we fail?" Tericia snaps, eyes hard.

"If he makes it up here?" Dave chimes in, standing near the window, trying not to sound as rattled as he is.

"Then he wins," Tericia finishes. "And we're either dead or stranded. Probably both. We'll have failed—not just ourselves, but the universe."

Lester's brow furrows. "Then let's strand him instead. Kill his return trip. Leave him choking on the dust."

"That would be nice," Tericia mutters, eyes narrowing. "But you remember what they say—'We don't take chances.' Makes me wonder how many backup exits he's got. Not to mention he is probably the only person who knows where the backup devices are."

"There can't be that many backups getting here, but we know where their ship is that allowed them access to this place. We can go and take it out," Parmen says. "Although, we need a ship or the vacuum of space will kill us."

Tericia nods. "Then we need three things. A ship. More fuel. And Tems—alive. We drag him back here and make that bastard talk."

Lester nods grimly. "And if we move fast enough, he should still be here, trapped like a rat."

"Alright," Tericia breathes, spinning toward Holepunch. "Let's go."

The device hums to life. A portal opens, revealing a spotless warehouse, floor gleaming like glass under overhead lights. Clean, silent—too perfect.

"You think they have Xomithrine here?" Lester asks, already doubting.

"They better," Tericia replies, flicking a switch on her weapon. "We don't have many options left."

"Parmen, stay here. If the portal closes, reopen it to this location," she instructs. "Lester and I know what we're looking for. Dave, you're on carry duty."

Dave salutes like a soldier finally getting picked for battle. "Yes, ma'am."

The three step through. Tericia tosses Dave a laser rifle on the way. His grin nearly splits his face.

They fan out, boots echoing down the sterile aisles, scanning for familiar labels. Tericia finds a locked container—big, solid, marked with all the proper hazard codes. She sets her weapon to low, then melts through the lock in seconds. The metal sizzles, slumps, and falls away.

She pushes the door open. Darkness yawns back at her. She steps in.

The lights snap on. The container is empty.

No Xomithrine. Not even residue.

Tericia's shoulders drop. She turns to Lester and shakes her head.

They step back out—only to hear a voice slice through the silence like a blade.

"You're not going to find any Xomithrine. Anywhere."

They turn fast.

Tems.

Standing there, calm. Smirking.

Dave doesn't hesitate—pulls the trigger and fires. The beam slices clean through Tems's midsection.

Tems doesn't flinch.

Lester fires again—straight through the face.

No blood. No reaction. No fall.

"Did you really think I'd make it that easy for you?" Tems's voice is smug, soaked in disdain.

Tericia walks up, hand extended. She waves her arm through him. Nothing but air.

"A fucking hologram," she growls. "An advanced one. Must've stolen it from some other brilliant scientist who is probably dead now."

"Stolen?" Tems echoes. "No, I paid well. More than I wanted to. But delivery was prompt—unlike you two."

"Real-time holographic technology," Lester mutters. "It's linked to wherever he actually is."

"And now," Tems continues, "I know exactly where you are. My decoy worked better than I hoped."

And then—he vanishes.

"Fuck!" Tericia snarls, sprinting back toward the wormhole.

Dave and Lester follow, weapons ready. Once they're through, Tericia slams the controls and kills the portal.

"We need to move," she pants. "Tems probably bought—or stole—every ounce of Xomithrine on Earth."

Lester turns to Dave. "Where was that abandoned place where we made the last batch?"

Dave frowns. "I'll tell you, but it won't be good. That place is crawling with desperate people now. You might not even recognize it. Very little chance that anything that you had there will still be there."

Tericia groans. "Fuck. He probably already tracked us on this planet while we were chasing his little decoy on Earth."

Parmen steps forward, firm and focused. "You handle fuel. I'll handle defenses. We'll be ready for whatever comes. Booby-traps are my favorite words."

"We need chemicals," Tericia says, nodding agreement toward Parmen, voice clipped. "Gear. Somewhere Tems wouldn't expect."

"Somewhere his goons won't think to check," Lester adds.

"Denver," he finally says. "Smaller than coastal cities, but still stocked. TeHg Elements should have everything."

"TeHg Elements it is. Let's move," Tericia says, keying in the coordinates.

Parmen nods and starts reinforcing the room as the others step through.

On the other side: shelves, tanks, beakers, gloves, goggles. The smell of solvents and metal.

Dave grabs the oversized glass globes used to store and process fuel, holding them like trophies. "I got these! I recognize them from the last time."

Lester smiles and nods at Dave. And then Lester and Tericia fan out through the aisles, sweeping up everything else they'll need. Chemicals, equipment, tubing—anything useful. They're in rhythm now. Like old times.

Back and forth they move. Hauling supplies, tossing them through the portal. Within minutes, a respectable pile takes shape inside their hideout.

Tericia heads toward the wormhole with one last armload. "This went better than expected. Should be able to make a lot of fuel—if we don't blow ourselves to hell."

Lester grins.

But then—a flash. The wormhole sputters. Whining.

"It's closing!" Tericia shouts.

Lester bolts.

"Stop!" she screams. "It's too unpredictable! It's going to close!"

But he doesn't stop. He's too close. Too stubborn.

The wormhole crackles again—seething on its edges. Tericia shuts her eyes, afraid to watch.

When she opens them, Lester is standing still. Alive. But the long metal tube he was carrying?

Gone. Sliced clean. Only a smoking end remains in his hand.

He stares at it, heart pounding.

"I told you," Tericia says, breathless.

"Now we wait for Parmen to reopen it," she mutters, glaring at the charred metal in Lester's hand.

He nods, still catching his breath. "That was… close."

CHAPTER 40

Lester paces the floor of the chemical supply warehouse, his steps sharp and restless. "It's been too long," he mutters, eyes flicking toward the dormant wormhole location like it might spring to life any second.

"I agree," Tericia replies, rising from her seat against the wall. Her movements are stiff—too many days of stress packed into too little sleep. "And the only way we know to get back there without our device is through Tems. Or, more specifically, his bastardized, cloned versions of it."

"But we don't know where those are," Lester says, stopping mid-pace to face her.

"No," Tericia replies, her brow furrowing. "And he doesn't know how to use ours since we modified the interface. Or the code to—" She stops, suddenly wide-eyed. "Shit." She slaps her forehead with her palm. "I know why Parmen can't get back here. I left the device unlocked, but I forgot I built in a failsafe. If I'm ever forcibly removed or too far from the device when a wormhole closes, it locks down."

Lester blinks. "And you didn't tell us the code?"

"I didn't exactly expect to be halfway across the galaxy without the damn thing ever again. Not to mention I am not thinking straight these days." She exhales. "The failsafe was for Tems—if he took me, it was supposed to lock him out."

"Well," Lester says, rubbing his jaw, "then I guess we've got ourselves a bargaining chip to get back to our device."

"Two, actually," Tericia says with a faint smirk only to have the smirk fade quickly.

Lester's face softens as well. He knows what she means. The unspoken words between them—hang in the air, heavy.

They step outside, leaving the shelter of the warehouse behind, and head toward a bustling intersection. Traffic hums. Cameras rotate. Drones zip overhead. Eyes are everywhere.

Finally, they flag down a taxi and climb inside.

"I really hope your plan's more than wishful thinking," Lester says, tension crawling into his voice.

"I have a plan," Tericia answers, her tone sharp. "I didn't say it was a good one."

"I'll take what I can get. The alternative is just…"

She looks over at him, studies his expression—the tight jaw, the darting eyes—and rests a hand gently on his leg. "Don't think about that. We'll get back. We'll find the devices. We'll find Tems. Together."

The ride feels longer than it is, every second dragging on Lester's nerves. No lock down. No security protocols engaged. When the taxi finally stops they exit the vehicle and head inside.

They step through the glass doors into a polished, echoing lobby.

"Interesting tactic," Tems says, standing tall on the other end of the lobby.

Tericia doesn't miss a beat. She marches forward and jabs both fingers into the eyes of Tems, which pass straight through.

"Had to be sure," she says, giving Lester a shrug. "I'm done playing it safe."

They continue forward until they reach a sleek waiting area. Tericia sits like she owns the room, crossing one leg over the other. Lester stays standing, watching the windows like they're war fronts.

"What are you doing?" the hologram asks.

"Waiting," Tericia replies, picking up a tablet from the table. "It is, after all, a waiting room."

"What game are you playing?" Tems demands.

"No games," Tericia answers without looking up. "You want something. We want something. Seems like a rare opportunity to work together."

The hologram fizzles and blinks out.

Tericia flips through headlines like she's reading the morning paper. Lester paces. Watches. Waits.

"Relax," she says finally. "He'll come. He loves his dramatic reveals."

"That's what I'm afraid of."

Outside, a fleet of blacked-out vehicles rolls into view, their wheels silent on the pavement. Lester's head jerks toward them.

"Here we go."

Tericia stands, smooth and unshaken. She walks to the door, opens it, and steps out like she's walking onto a red carpet. The laser rifles pointed at her don't even register in her expression.

"Which one do you want us to get in?" she asks, smiling like a queen meeting her escort.

Lester hovers close behind, sweat dampening his collar.

"Separate vehicles," one of the guards announces.

Without hesitation, Tericia draws her weapon and blasts him point-blank in the face. The man drops to the ground into a lump.

"As I said," Tericia repeats, her voice like ice. "Which vehicle do you want US to get in?"

Another guard stutters, "We were told to—"

She shoots him too.

"We both know you've been told to bring us in alive. So I'll stand here and keep blowing holes in faces until you grow a spine and point to a damn car."

The rest of the guards—now wide-eyed and pale—point at random vehicles. All of them.

Tericia turns to Lester. "Looks like we get to pick."

She holsters her weapon, links her arm in his, and walks toward the sleek black transport at the front of the convoy like nothing just happened.

They walk together, arm in arm—partners, rebels, and the biggest damn threat Borvil's ever underestimated.

CHAPTER 41

Tems storms toward Tericia the moment she steps out of the vehicle and slams the butt of his pistol across her face. Her head jerks sideways from the blow, blood flaring in her mouth. She spits a thick glob onto the pavement, straightens up, and wipes her cheek with the back of her hand, smearing the blood into a crimson streak.

"Good to see the actual you for once," she says, voice cool, defiant. "The holograms were getting pathetic."

Tems's nostrils flare. "I told them not to kill you," he growls, leaning in close. "But I didn't say anything about keeping you intact."

"And you saw how well that worked out last time," Tericia bites back, her tone sharp and unshaken.

Tems sneers. "That was just a ruse. A brilliant one, too. You weren't talking, and I needed results."

Behind her, Lester lets out a sneeze—sharp, badly timed, and loud enough to draw every eye.

Tems turns toward him slowly, eyes narrowing. "Maybe lover boy here's more cooperative," he says, pulling out his gun and leveling it at Lester's face. "Or maybe you'll start talking when I blow his fucking head off."

Tericia steps in front of the weapon, calm but deliberate. "I wouldn't do that," she warns. "Not unless you want to lose everything."

Tems pauses. His hand doesn't lower, but he doesn't shoot either. There's a flicker of doubt in his eyes—brief, but enough.

"Let me make this simple," Tericia says, arms crossed now, chin held high. "You and I both want access to my machine. For very different reasons. Unfortunately for both of us, I locked the controls. That's why I'm here. That's why I need your help."

"You need my help?" Tems scoffs. "Why the hell would I take you back to that planet? Why would I willingly walk into a trap?"

"You don't have a choice," Tericia says evenly. "I know your jump points. I know how this works. Your first wormhole device is close, right? You've got a ship. All we need is a ride."

Tems's eyes go dead cold. His expression doesn't change—but the fury in his jaw says it all. Without a word, he cracks her across the face again with the pistol. Harder this time.

"Take them to the ship," he barks to the guards. "Now."

The guards seize them by the arms and drag them across the tarmac toward the vessel. Lester keeps his head low. Tericia barely reacts. Her smile, cracked and bloodied, is still there.

A few minutes later, Tems boards the ship in full armor— military grade, jet-black with reactive plating and servo joints that hiss with each step. Weapons bristle from every corner of his frame. The gold detailing on his rifle glints under the hangar lights. It's excessive. Showy. Exactly what you'd expect from a narcissist with power.

He drops into the seat across from them, fingers resting on the barrel of his rifle.

"Get us to the entrance. Now," he barks to the pilot.

The ship lifts off, and the engines hum with precision. Tems doesn't even look out the window. His eyes lock on Tericia and Lester.

"As soon as I get that machine, you're both dead," he says, flat and final.

Tericia leans back against the wall, arms still bound. "No, we're not."

Tems's lip curls. "You keep saying that. Like I give a shit."

"You do," she replies. "You trained us. You beat it into our heads."

Tems raises an eyebrow. "Beat what into your heads?"

Her grin sharpens. "We don't take chances."

That line hangs between them like a trigger.

Tems doesn't answer. He doesn't blink. He just stares—calculating, unreadable.

And Tericia just smiles wider, even as the blood from her split lip trickles down her chin.

Tems's ship emerges from the final wormhole and glides over Planet Vista's skies.

"Where to?" he barks from his seat, impatience dripping from his voice.

"The tall building near the center of the city," Tericia says evenly. "Land there. We walk."

Tems glares through the viewport. "Which fucking city? There are thousands."

"Oh? I thought you said you knew where our base was," Tericia mocks, her smirk taunting. "I guess you're full of shit."

Tems stands, eyes burning, and backhands her with the butt of his pistol—again. She grunts, blood flying from her lip, but remains strong in composure.

"Fuck, Tems!" Lester shouts. "Leave her alone! We only ever arrived by wormhole. We don't know which city! We didn't know there were more than one!"

Without hesitation, Tems strides over and slams the butt of his pistol into Lester's skull. Lester drops like a stone.

"Looks like your boyfriend's glass-jawed," Tems sneers. "Want to see if I can knock you out too?"

Tericia doesn't flinch. "Fuck you," she spits, literally, blood landing on his boot.

Tems grins. "If I didn't want to kill you so badly, I'd say we'd make the perfect couple—defiant, unhinged, mouthy."

"And if we were a couple, I'd cut your dick off while you slept and ram it down your fucking throat. Just to hear you gurgle on your own blood," Tericia snarls.

Tems stares at her for a long beat. Then, "Pilot! Take us city by city. Tallest building in each."

"You'll know when we get there," Tericia says. "Trust me—I want that device even more than you do."

City after city blurs past. Finally, the eighth one lights a fire in Tericia's memory.

"That's it," she says. "Let me up—I need to be sure."

Tems cuts her restraints with a combat knife, slicing a thin line into her arm as he does. Blood trickles down.

She glares at him, then deliberately smears the blood down his armored chest plate.

Stepping toward the front viewport, she studies the skyline, then points. "There. Land in front of the building."

As she walks back, she reaches toward Tems's chest and slips a knife from his utility strap. Tems recoils just as she turns to Lester and slices his restraints free.

She tosses the knife over her shoulder—missing Tems by a hair. She grunts a sound of disapproval at missing Tems.

Lester groans as she kneels beside him. "It's time. Can you stand?"

"I can walk," Lester murmurs, swaying as he pushes himself up.

"If not, we'll drag your ass," Tems growls.

Tericia, Lester, Tems and a couple of guards disembark and walk the path toward the massive building's entrance.

The architecture looms above, clean, alien, and disturbingly familiar.

"What floor?" Tems demands.

"The top. But I've never taken the lobby route before," Tericia replies as they walk through the entrance.

"Fucking useless," Tems mutters. "Guards—find a stairwell or elevator."

As the guards fan out, Lester eyes the towering structures around them. "Weird, isn't it? How much this place looks like Earth?"

"I don't give a shit," Tems says. "I just want my profits to soar."

Tericia wanders slightly, catching a blinking red light in the corner. Surveillance. She makes a show of heading the opposite direction to draw Tems's attention.

"Found stairs!" a guard shouts.

"Good. Move out!" Tems barks.

Moments later—a boom rattles the walls. Dust rains from the ceiling.

Tericia smiles sweetly. "Oops."

"What the fuck was that?" Tems blurts out, anger and fear showing in his stance.

"Booby trap?" Tericia surmises with a shrug. "Guess we wait here and die. Your move."

"Go find them!" Tems shouts to the second guard. "And watch for traps!"

"Oh, look at you—concerned about someone other than yourself for a change?" Tericia mocks.

"Fuck no. I just need him to get as far as your hideout," Tems says. "In the meantime, come with me."

"Where are we going?" she asks.

"Back to the ship. We'll land on the roof."

"I really wouldn't do that," Tericia warns. "We stole a lot of nasty toys. Parmen probably has the roof wired with anti-air systems."

Tems's jaw tightens, his temper waning. "You didn't plan for this very well, did you?"

"Didn't think we would have been separated from my device, no," Tericia admits. "But, I can make an educated guess as to what you should do. Lower your weapons and surrender. Then, Parmen can let us up to the top floor and..."

Another boom shudders the stairwell. Gunfire cracks. Then silence.

"...and there goes your last guard," she adds.

A beep emits from Tems's suit. He grins. "What were you telling me I have taught you?" Tems winks and exits the building.

"Parmen, if you can see me... he's planning something big," Tericia says to the blinking light in the corner.

"Should we follow him?" Lester asks.

"I will. But you wait here. Head to the top floor. If you make it to the top—here's the code," she whispers in his ear.

He looks at her and grabs her gently on the shoulders and moves in for a kiss as he says, "I love you."

"Uhh…I like the sentiment, but my face is swollen and anything that touches it will make it hurt," Tericia says. "And…I love you too."

Tericia heads outside to catch up to Tems. She finds him staring up at the sky.

Fighter ships descend.

"Tall building! Watch for anti-air! Clear the roof!" Tems commands while looking skyward.

"You destroy the roof, you lose what you came for!" Tericia warns.

Tems doesn't miss a beat. "Leave the top floor intact!" he finishes. "Happy, you fucking bitch?"

"No. You're still breathing," Tericia says, pulling a knife and driving it into his gut.

Tems buckles over from the shock of something hitting him, but he doesn't fall. He looks down and sees the knife. He punches his hands down, knocking the knife out of Tericia's hands and then hits her in the face with the butt end of the rifle he is carrying.

She hits the ground hard. She sees the knife skitter by. No blood.

"Did you think you could cut through this material?" Tems says as he kicks Tericia in the side. "I won't kill you, but I am going to make you wish you were dead."

The sound of weapons fire rings down from the sky. Tericia hears it just moments before Tems jumps up and lands with both legs on hers, snapping bone.

A boom from above, masking her screams. A fighter, shot down.

Tems kneels down and grabs Tericia's arm. He places it over his cybernetic knee and then jerks down hard, snapping her forearm.

Another loud boom, another fighter down, another masking of her screams. "Roof's clear. Copy," Tems says into his comm.

He drags her, broken and bloodied, back to the ship. Each step he takes is an agonizing eternity for Tericia. The pain floods her body.

"Take us to the roof," Tems commands, his pilot nods.

The ship lands on the rooftop moments later. Tems yanks Tericia out, dragging her by her only good arm. Soldiers sprint past them—dozens. Their ships having landed just moments before.

A trio reaches the door.

It explodes outward—flinging them off the roof like ragdolls.

More charge in. The first gets dropped instantly.

A grenade flies inside—BOOM.

Tericia's screams muffle the sounds of war, but only for herself and Tems, who draws closer to the entrance. The soldiers file through the door, popping sounds and explosions moving deeper into the building.

At last, Tems lets go of Tericia's arm. He holds his rifle and looks through the door and peers down as far as he can. He sees flashing. Small arms fire and larger explosions. Parmen standing tall against many soldiers.

After a while, the noise stops. Tems stands silent. He walks back out to the roof to grab Tericia. Before he can make contact, Dave comes running and slams into Tems, throwing him against the door, and falling to the ground. Dave stands up as quickly as he can and draws his gun, aiming at Tems's body.

Tericia attempts to say something important. Her body, unable to move as she wants. Her face, swollen shut can't make out words. She reaches out with her good arm only to see Dave's eyes go wide. Tems pulls the trigger of a small weapon he had stored in his suit while Dave is smiling at his accomplishment. Dave, who tried to save Tericia, a man who just wanted to live life and try something new, shot in the stomach for doing something stupid and failing at his rescue attempt. An overzealous man thinking this reality was an easy one to navigate.

Tems stands and returns to Tericia. "He could have shot me. It would have hurt. But it wouldn't have gone through the armor," Tems says, pulling Tericia by her good arm, making sure she knew that Dave never had a chance.

Tems drags Tericia down each step with a thud. Her body bruising more with each step. Screams no longer making noise as she is too weak to breath.

Parmen appears through the doorway as Tems reaches the next floor down.

Parmen sees Tericia, Tems, and notices Dave isn't with them.

"Your boy is dead. Tried to kill me. I guess you didn't tell him not to try," Tems says. "Now stand aside or you will be joining him."

"Let him through," Lester says, catching his breath from climbing the stairs.

Parmen pivots to see Lester coming up the stairs.

Tericia nods to Parmen, her only way to communicate and Parmen backs through the door. He doesn't lower his weapon and nor does Tems.

"I don't suppose I can't kill him like I can't kill you two?" Tems asks, looking at Parmen while asking Lester.

"Based on the outfits, I am guessing it would be a stalemate," Lester says. "So, let's figure out our next steps," Lester continues as he walks through the door, waiting for Tems to bring Tericia through.

As he does, he drops her arm and looks around. Lester runs up to Tericia and helps her up onto her good leg, and moves her to their bed.

Tems and Parmen maintain tactical positions, while Tems looks around their stronghold. He finally finds the device and smiles.

"Finally," he whispers.

CHAPTER 42

"Make it work!" Tems snarls, slamming his palm against the console after yet another failed attempt.

"Can't," Lester says, calm but firm. "She added a code. That's why we got stuck back on Earth. She never told anyone she locked it down."

"He's telling the truth," Parmen adds, eyes trained on Tems through the scope of his rifle. "We couldn't reopen it because of her failsafe."

Tems turns to the unconscious Tericia. "Then wake her up and get the code!"

"Not until you give us the location of every cloned device," Lester says, rising from his seat.

"Fuck you and fuck that! I have plans for those! Once I break this thing down, I'll own the fucking universe. Now GIVE ME THE FUCKING CODE!" Tems roars.

"Why are we keeping this asshole alive again?" Parmen asks, fingers flexing over the trigger.

"Because he's the only one who knows where the clones are," Lester replies.

"Someone else has to know," Parmen counters.

"No. He's too paranoid. He probably killed anyone who got too close to the truth," Lester says. "That's what he'd do to us too, the moment he got what he wanted."

"He's not wrong," Tems says with a grin.

"Tell me there's another way to find them," Parmen mutters. "Say the word, and I'll end him now."

Lester steps up, leans in close to whisper something to Parmen. Then he moves slowly between Tems and the device.

"What the fuck do you want?" Tems snaps.

"I'm actually glad you knocked her out," Lester says, removing his jacket and letting it drop.

"Getting tired of her bullshit too?" Tems smirks.

"No," Lester says evenly. "I love her. More than you could ever comprehend. But she'd never let me do what has to be done."

He takes a deep breath, then shoves Tems in the chest. Tems staggers slightly but recovers.

"She'd beg me to stop this," Lester says, shoving Tems again—harder this time. "She wouldn't want me to provoke you."

"What the hell are you even trying?" Tems scoffs.

Lester steps forward again, shoving harder.

"She'd say it wasn't worth it," Lester growls. Then he swings a fist—Tems easily deflects and counters with a punch to Lester's stomach. He doubles over, gasping.

While catching his breath, Lester palms a small metal object off the ground and swings, cracking it against Tems's helmet. No effect.

"Seriously? You're pathetic," Tems growls. He bats the object away with the butt of his rifle.

Lester lunges forward again, pushing Tems toward the window. Tems sidesteps and lets him stumble past.

"This is just sad," Tems says, confused but amused.

Lester gets to his feet—this time holding a pistol.

Tems eyes it. "What are you going to do, shoot me?"

"No," Lester says. "I'm going to tell you why you can't shoot me."

Tems laughs. "Please, enlighten me."

"If I die, my body sends a signal. Every cloned device you've made will detonate. All of the code will erase itself. Every trace of your stolen empire gone in a heartbeat."

"Bullshit," Tems sneers. "We'd never build that into the system."

"You would if you copied us," Lester replies. "And you said you did."

"No way. We'd have seen it."

"You would've. If you hadn't hired idiots who just mirrored our designs. People who didn't understand what they were building."

"You don't know that."

"I do," Lester says. "Because the only people who did know were in that room with me. And you killed every last one of them."

Tems says nothing.

"Oh. Believe me when I say that it took a lot of work to figure out chemical compounds that seemed accurate for wormholes and the mechanics of the system only to use them against you when and if you decided my time was up. New explosives that haven't existed until you came along," Lester continues.

"So, you don't even know if the explosives work," Tems smiles.

"Yeah. We do. We tested it. And, if you remember the fire alarm trick we pulled, well, we lied. It wasn't to see if we could actually get out and feel fresh air. It was to test our explosive solution. It worked. It worked too well. We lost a colleague testing that solution," Lester says, taking another step toward Tems.

"I'm calling bullshit," Tems says, brushing aside Lester.

"You know Tems, you have taught me well over the years. There is no way you will give away the locations of your devices. No matter what we say, do, agree on, or anything. You'll always be killing us in the end," Lester says. "It might just be better if you did. Maybe I should just kill myself now."

Tems eyes narrow. "You're bluffing."

"I guess you'll know in a second," Lester says. And he puts the barrel under his chin—and pulls the trigger.

The shot rings out.

Parmen doesn't hesitate. He opens fire on Tems, hitting him in the neck, the weakest point in the armor. He sees Tems fall, and rushes over, putting the muzzle against Tems's chin. He releases round after round into Tems's helmet. A red spray covering the inside of the helmet and nothing more to see of Tems.

In the doorway, Tericia appears—dragging herself forward. Her body broken, her eyes wide with grief.

She sees Lester's body. A sob escapes as she collapses.

She crawls, bloodied fingers clawing across the floor, trying to get to Lester until Parmen lifts her gently, bringing her to Holepunch.

"You know what you have to do," Parmen says quickly. "Lester told me you would know."

Tericia nods. She knows that she needs to open a wormhole to Earth to get Lester's loss of life signal to Earth's communications systems. Only then will the other devices explode, the code erased, and the technology burned from existence. Only then will Borvil have nothing.

"I'll be right back. Wait two minutes," Parmen says, then bolts from the room.

Tericia taps in the code with shaking hands. A wormhole blossoms open—to a hospital, white walls glowing through the portal. She can get the help she needs and get the signal out.

The staff in the hospital stand in awe, seeing this battered woman on the other side of a glowing doorway.

Moments later, Parmen reappears, carrying Dave in his arms. He walks through the wormhole, lays him on a gurney and races back to Tericia.

He helps her and the device through. She stumbles—and falls.

"Don't just stand there—help her!" Parmen shouts at the stunned medical staff.

EPILOGUE

Tericia stands alone at the edge of a lake, its waters tinted a deep crimson beneath the light of the red star above. The surface shimmers like molten glass, disturbed only by the wind. In her hands, she cradles an urn. Tears well in her eyes but don't fall—not yet.

"I've gotten confirmation," she says softly to the breeze, "that this lake is now officially named Lake Lester." Her voice trembles. "It was the least they could do after everything that happened."

She twists off the lid, slowly, reverently. The first gust takes a thin veil of ashes across the wind. Then she tips the urn fully, letting the last of Lester fall, grain by grain, into the alien waters that now carry his name.

"Why didn't you let me find another way?" she whispers, almost angry. "I wanted you here. When it was over. When we could be scientists again."

Footsteps crunch along the path behind her.

Parmen slows as he approaches, stopping a respectful distance away. "How's your farewell ceremony going?" he asks gently.

Without answering, Tericia caps the urn and wipes her face with the sleeve of her jacket. She brushes past him on the path.

"I'm sorry I had to interrupt," he says as they fall into step.

"It's fine. I knew I didn't have much time."

The two climb into a hover cart and glide in silence back toward their headquarters, nestled in the foothills overlooking what was once a ghost city—and is now the most secure and advanced research hub in known space.

Inside, Holepunch is now sealed in an armored chamber lined with defensive systems, glass thicker than tank armor, and automated sentries hanging like wasps from the ceiling.

Tericia steps forward and inputs her code. The wormhole pulses open, revealing a portal to Earth. On cue, five scientists step through—each previously vetted, approved, and triple-confirmed. Tericia holds her hand over the close button. Beside her, Parmen hovers over the abort switch—his finger never far from ending the new arrivals instantly.

Once the last scientist is through, she seals the wormhole. Each visitor is scanned, catalogued, and briefed by Dave—now fully recovered and serving as their head of logistics and security review. He checks their belongings thoroughly ensuring nothing that wasn't already authorized gets through.

His once-boyish excitement has matured into something steadier, more focused.

"You're cleared for exploration," Dave says, handing a digital wristband to the final newcomer. "Your assignments and working parameters are embedded in them."

Only three people are allowed inside the control chamber: Tericia, Parmen, and Dave. Together, they are the gatekeepers to Planet Vista.

"Think we'll ever explore other systems?" Parmen asks as the latest batch of scientists departs into the field.

"Probably," Tericia replies. "But first, we need real governance around this tech. Until Earth stops fighting over power they can't even reach, we're only allowing scientists. People focused on discovery, not domination."

"And what happens when we get tired of guarding the galaxy's front door?" Parmen asks. "When we've had enough?"

"I haven't decided," Tericia says quietly. "Maybe I take Holepunch and vanish into the stars. Let Earth bicker itself into dust."

"I'd go," Parmen says with a grin. "Babysitting power-hungry Earthlings isn't as glamorous as it sounds."

Dave walks up, arms folded, half-smiling. "Count me in. I didn't sign up for politics—I signed up for the stars."

Tericia nods. "Lester would've wanted that, too. To see what's out there. To build something better."

"He gave his life for this," Parmen says, his voice hardening. "Don't let grief rewrite that."

"I won't," Tericia replies. "There really was no other way. And if I had to choose again, I'd still choose us."

They step outside as the red sun dips low on the horizon.

"Let's rest up," Parmen says. "Tomorrow's going to be full of posturing and begging."

"All those Earth dignitaries thinking they can twist our arms," Dave adds with a scoff.

"They've got power back there," Tericia says, smiling. "But here? We decide who gets through. That has to piss them off."

"Let them be pissed," Parmen says, chuckling as the building's doors close behind them.

As a Matter of Effect

By Ben Winter

Other books by Ben Winter: https://mrimprov.com